HITTAZ 5

Everybody Suspect

LOU GARDEN PRICE, SR.

URBAN AINT DEAD

Contact Author at: paralegal.louprice2@gmail.com

Snail mail: LOU GARDEN PRICE SBI 00454309

Delaware DOC 1101

PO Box 96777

Las Vegas Nevada 89193

**See: GettingOut.com/create account

Search Lou Garden Price SBI #00454309

James T Vaughn Correctional Center, Smyrna DELAWARE

For tablet connection. Download the gettingout.com app.

Contact Publisher at www.urbanaintdead.com

Email: urbanaintdead@gmail.com

Print ISBN: 979-8-9902387-9-4

STAY UP TO DATE

To stay up to date on new releases, plus get information on contests,
sneak peaks and more,
Click the link below...
https://mailchi.mp/6d21003686d1/subscribe

CONTENTS

<u>Soundtracks</u>

Scan the QR Code below to listen to the Soundtracks/Singles of some of your favorite U.A.D titles:

Don't have Spotify or Apple Music?
No Sweat!
Visit your choice streaming platform and search URBAN AINT DEAD.

Currently on lock serving a bid?
JPay, iHeartRadio, WHATEVER!
We got you covered.

Simply log into your facility's kiosk or tablet, go to music and search URBAN AINT DEAD.

URBAN AINT DEAD

Like & Follow us on social media:
FB - URBAN AINT DEAD
IG: @urbanaintdead
Tik Tok - @urbanaintdead

<u>Submissions</u>

Submit the first three chapters of your completed manuscript to
<u>urbanaintdead@gmail.com</u>, subject line: Your book's title. The
manuscript must be in a .doc file and sent as an attachment. The
document should be in Times New Roman, double-spaced, and in size
12 font. Also, provide your synopsis and full contact information. If
sending multiple submissions, they must each be in a separate email.
Have a story but no way to submit it electronically? You can still
submit to URBAN AINT DEAD. Send in the first three chapters,
written or typed, of your completed manuscript to:

URBAN AINT DEAD
P.O Box 448
Maybrook, NY 12543

DO NOT send original manuscript. Must be a duplicate.
Provide your synopsis and a cover letter containing your full contact
information.
Thanks for considering URBAN AINT DEAD.

ACKNOWLEDGMENTS

Thank you Lord for your grace and the time you've allowed me to borrow.

Those who are closest to me I thank you all for the support received following the death of my pops.

Big love and respect to my Brooklyn homie "OGIZZAL" owner/CEO of KITE magazine. Your book "Understanding The Misunderstood" ain't just some ordinary self-help joint, but I got energy from it that I never thought I had. Real deep – and watch what I tell you son. Ya grandkids gonna come and say how much it helps them, son.

Thank you to all of my readers for making all of my books a favorite. And so highly rated. I just love to do what I've done since 1987. I work long and hard hours so y'all can always count on genuine work 100%. Not that fake ass artificial intelligence bullshit these brand-new false authors will start coming out the woodwork with. There are apps to find out if you are buying A.I. bullshit (You won't get a nickel of mine).

Alyssa Jade Popo–hey pretty lady. I ain't forgetcha! To everyone else…

One.

Lou Garden Price, SR.
Ighostwritebooks523@gmail.com

PART ONE

Don't take my kindness for weakness. I am kind to everyone but when someone is unkind to me, weak is not what you are going to remember about me.

-Al Capone

CHAPTER ONE

At the very moment the $4 million-dollar Bugatti Chiron Super Sport lost control, Joker Red knew he was fucked. The Everything is Everything or (EIE) mercenary leader was not a NASCAR driver inside of a vehicle that had been built to withstand just about any kind of crash - - including rollover impact- - and he wasn't about to be a living crash test dummy for the Chiron either.

Joker was an apex predator – like a wolf or a lion. That meant he did not and could not freeze up in the face of death. He had taken heavy gunfire from his blindside and one of the bullets, probably a .223 round, had struck him in the upper right back and exited through the right shoulder. But, still, instinct was a God-given spirit or quality of survival.

When the pricey luxury car spun out Joker had less than a tenth of a second to decide whether he would stay inside of the out-of-control four-million-dollar "soda can" or jump out and take his chances on the land. It was never even a decision. It was an extremely fast, daredevil act that could have killed him. In fact, it should have killed him – but it didn't.

The door swung open, he was out of his safety belt, and he didn't necessarily "jump" from the car, he tumbled out of it as it spun in a

360-degree circle and did a wild flip sideways. That first flip added more momentum and speed to the second flip which was over a guard rail and down into a grassy ravine.

Meanwhile, Joker's body had been thrown as he'd escaped the vehicle. He ended up about fifteen to twenty feet down in a ditch right off of that winding right turn at the Winthrop Exit. He was having trouble breathing because of the gunshot wound and multiple injuries he suffered during the jump and crushing landing.

While he struggled to breathe he kept thinking the Albanian hittaz inside of that Charger would come to finish him off. It was true that the black Charger had paused to observe the Chiron and the catastrophic condition it was in. But seeing no sign of life and a fuel leak from its tank engulf it into a growing fire, they sped off. Apparently, they had missed Joker's body being sling-shotted out of the doomed Chiron.

"Fuck!" Joker whispered as he slowly regained his eyesight.

A white man dressed in overalls carefully eased his way down the dew slick crab grass followed by two young boys who could be no older than 13 and 14. The two scraggly kids were also dressed in overalls and plaid shirts. Joker would later learn that the Father, Bill Osterman, was a farm owner and it was actually his sons who had seen Joker get thrown from the Bugatti while they were returning from a bank in Chicago.

"Mister, mister!" Farmer Bill said as calmly as he could. He had never seen anything like this. First there was one overturned car, a little ways back from where they were now. And now this. "Oh, Lordy, Paul and Jake, he's alive!"

The two boys came closer.

"Can you walk?" The farmer asked kindly. He looked at Joker's legs. "Just let me get a look."

Joker nodded at him. "Is my phone in my pocket?" He asked the man.

The farmer searched through Joker's pants pocket and pulled out a stack of $100 bills about an inch thick. Joker seen something in his eyes.

"You help me out of here and I'll return the favor," Joker told him. "*Before* cops arrive."

"Is that a bullet wound?" The man asked.

"We don't have time to talk!" Joker replied, trying to stand up but the pain was too great. He had broken ribs. "Please, sir!"

"Come on, boys," Farmer Bill ordered his sons. "Let's get 'into the truck!"

They lifted Joker up and helped him up the hill as he grunted and groaned in agonizing pain. The farmer was driving an older white Silverado. They put the wounded man in the back of the truck where Joker laid down on the filthy bed of the vehicle, menacing in pain.

"Where to? You need a hospital!" The farmer suggested.

"Your house," Joker said in a grimace.

The man was hesitant. "This can be a lot of trouble for me. I don't want no troubles!"

With that he hopped inside of his truck and drove away only a minute before first responders reached the crash sites.

CHAPTER TWO

The Osterman Farm
Richmond, IL
2:30 AM

It was dark when he woke up. Joker looked around and deduced that he was inside of a small camper. He looked down at his body underneath the sheet and blanket he'd been covered with and saw that all he had on were his boxers and socks. He had been given a soapy wash and his bullet wounds had been bandaged up nicely. The farmer must have given him something for the pain because he could barely feel anything.

Except when he sat up. He did a self-check and thought he had broken three ribs on his left side. It hurt to breathe when he was sitting so he got out of bed and looked around for his clothes. He couldn't locate them, but he did see an old pair of overalls with a black plaid shirt. He sniffed them first before putting them on. They were fresh.

He exited the silver ten-foot camper and an English sheepdog barked and met him at the door. Seconds later, a larger sheepdog approached, wagging its ass because this breed of sheepdog had no tail.

Both dogs were happy to see him for some reason. Maybe they were lonely.

Joker limped a few feet away from the camper, taking in where he was at. To his left was a chicken coop but at least ten of the chickens were out and about, wandering around. An old rusted-out tractor sat next to the coop. Up ahead about fifteen feet was a barn. He followed the dirt road around a bend and saw the small farmhouse with the older model Silverado that he had been transported to the farm in parked outside of it. The lights in the house were out.

He knocked on the front door and wondered what time it was and even more importantly where he was at. He recalled asking the farmer where his cell phone was but couldn't find it. Injuries or not, he couldn't be immobile. Not with the treacherous enemies he had coming out of the woodwork at him. He had heads to chop off.

The light on the front porch came on and the door opened. The white farmer pushed the screen door outward and stepped aside.

"What time is it?" Joker inquired as he came in.

"Two-thirty AM," the farmer informed him. "My wife and boys are asleep so…"

It smelled like beans and collard greens were cooking inside of the house. There was the permanent aroma of cooked food that hung in the air inside of the cozy little ranch-style home. Joker was led into the living room where he sat down on a rust-colored cloth sofa that had seen better days.

On the homemade wooden coffee table was Joker's washed and dried clothing that he'd been wearing during the crash. Beside his clothes was the cash that had been inside of his pocket as well as a burner phone.

"I thought I lost this," Joker said aloud, picking up the phone and the stack of $100 bills. "The money is yours. There's five grand there but you've taken great risk so whatever you need or want, I got you."

"Well, Ole Bill been fixin' on that junk piece'uh tractor out thar for f'eva," a woman in her forties drawled as she came out wrapped tightly in a yellow wool robe. She put another log on the fire in the fireplace. "He an' the boys were on thar way from the city today but… as usual the banks turned us away. Thar's just no way to maintain a farm and then still try to compete at the market wit' inflation the way it's been under these goddamned Democrats."

"Sir, this is my wife, Betty Sue from Little Rock, Arkansas," Bill introduced by extended his hand. "We's all from Lil Rock 'cept the boys. Her daddy–Mr. Lindy–gave her the farm twenty years ago. He taught me everything I know til' he passed. I'm William Osterman – best known as Farmer Bill."

"Nice to meet you, ma'am," Joker Red nodded her way. "You bandaged me up?"

She nodded. "You are one banged up fellar. Ya ribs are busted in."

"You not scared of blood?"

She shook her head. "Can't own a farm and be scared of blood. You got a name?"

"Just call me Red," he told her as he sent a text out to Vinnie: *My own doctor-girl tried poisoning me. But there is an even bigger conspiracy goin' on wit the Albanians and a Victoria Linze... We need to meet. But dust must settle after the highway incident earlier. Watch the news. I'll contact you soon. Ghostman is not to be trusted. Honey B not to be trusted.*

Joker sent that same text to the rest of his organization, letting them know that he was alive and well. When they all crashed his burner phone at the same time with inquisitive-toned text messages he sent out a group text telling everyone to gather at The Twin Towers for an emergency meeting in the War Room the following afternoon.

"Where's the farm located at?" Joker asked the Osterman couple. "Winthrop Harbor?"

Bill shook his head. "No. Winthrop is more like an upper-class area, the water, boats, and restaurants. We're located up along the Wisconsin border in Richmond."

"All farms out here?"

"A few," Bill answered. "Ours is mainly sheep."

I need an armored vehicle in Richmond- NOW, he texted Bible. *Let Leah know to bring my encrypted phone and a suitcase full of cash. Bring reinforcements, tac gear, weapons. Stay on high alert.*

Bill provided exact directions to the farm and then they waited.

"Ma'am," Joker said as Mrs. Osterman gave him coffee, a slice of apple pie, and a fork. "Thank you and your husband for everything. My people are on their way."

The woman went back to bed.

Bill stayed up with Joker Red.

CHAPTER THREE

The Osterman Farm
Richmond, ILL

It was after 5:00 AM when three black Cadillac SUVs barreled down the main dirt road which led them directly to the farmhouse. Inside, Joker had been locked onto the internet, searching for news updates while waiting for his team to arrive. Farmer Bill had nodded off on the sofa.

Joker put his burner phone away and went outside to meet his people. Eustace "Bible" Reed was first to step out of the Cadillac which was driven by one of Joker's 13 women, Leah. Bible was probably the most humble and loyal friend Joker had right now.

Bible said nothing but he walked up to Joker and hugged him tightly, knocking the breath out of Joker due to his injuries.

"I'm wounded!" Joker gasped in pain.

"I'll kill 'em all, Red!" Bible vowed. "In the name of Christ Jesus, the Master and King – I'll kill 'em all or die tryin'."

Joker patted the 6 feet 5-inch, 320-pound, gargantuan man on his shoulder. "My dearest friend and Bishop Warrior, I know for a fact that you would. And we will if you don't kill me first! You don't know your strength, son."

Leah gently hugged him, and she had tears in her eyes as she affectionately kissed him. He used both thumbs to wipe the tears away as they fell. He pulled the 5 feet 6 inch bleached blond closer to him and truly appreciated all that she did. He looked into her sparkling blue eyes and pretty round face and knew she was one of a kind. She was not only a dime piece with a banging body that had curves for days and had become his premiere communications/logistics/online and dark net specialist. The remarkable thing about Leah's skills was that she was self-taught. She could hack into major networks, cause chaos, create viruses, and much more. She was very valuable to EIE as a whole now. Not just to Joker.

"We get everything done down in Florida yet?" Joker asked her.

He was referring to the organization's Central Intelligence Network (CIN). EIE, Inc. had secured a lease for a four-story building inside of an obscure office complex in West Palm Beach, Florida. They had also leased a temporary mega mansion there owned by a billionaire businessman who was getting divorced from his R& B superstar wife following allegations of her steamy affair with her plastic surgeon.

"The girls are down there," Leah filled him in.

"All of them?"

She nodded. "The kids, too. You already know that Uzenna, Baby Joker One, his nanny Amelia, Coral, Ashley, Eden, Val, Iani, Britt, and myself were there. Lieutenant Sampson Gates supplied security like you asked…like a small army. I didn't count. Ceasar and Breach are here with Bible, me, Casci Caliendo… and Nina."

Joker greeted the others. Casci gave him a duffel bag. He went inside to get dressed in black tactical clothing and boots. He retrieved the specialized encrypted cell phone and re-entered the living room where the fire warmed them all up. Inside of the large duffle bag was a small briefcase that contained $50,000.

"This is our new friend, Farmer Bill," Joker said, introducing him. "Nina...?"

The five feet nine-inch-tall good-looking dark chocolate CIA agent came forward. "Hey, man. Glad you're still in one piece. That four-million-dollar car is like a can that got crushed by Thor's Hammer. They saw it on TV, freaked out, and called me to see what I could find out. Leah had a heart attack."

Leah, still emotional at the close call he'd had with *death*, walked away before she broke apart in tears again. It was scary.

He looked over in Leah's direction. "Well… she has a long, long history of people doin' bad things to her, losin' people she cares about… no one could imagine what she been through."

"I felt like I lost my world for a minute," Casci blurted. "I mean the panic caved my chest in, man!"

Joker embraced the tall, leggy, Colombian woman with the sandy brown hair and aqua-green eyes. "But you are a combat solider who knows that death is a part of this life. Dyin' and killin' are what we do. Plus, the bank account ain't bad, right?" He smiled that sinister smile of his, drawing chuckles across the group.

He gave Nina the 50k he held in the suitcase and said to the farmer, "She's goin' to explain the importance of silence to you about us, Farmer Bill. The cash is for anything you need it for. Maybe a tractor. Y'all take care of yourselves ya heard?"

"You got it, bud. You too." They shook hands.

Joker climbed into the lead Caddy which Leah drove. She sat up front alone while Bible sat in the rear with Joker Red. They waited for Nina Overstreet to return from speaking with Bill and his family about national security ramifications of anything they saw or heard or know about Joker and the highway incident.

"The FBI has full command over the highway crime scene," Nina informed him. "I just knew some crazy shit was about to happen after that mess the Indian girl pulled. That's why I put Maxine Crawford on alert."

Maxine was the Department of Defense official who was linked up with CIA Agent Nina Overstreet to handle Joker Red and EIE missions they were ordered on.

"What she haveta say?" Joker queried.

"To be ready to play clean up," Nina said nonchalantly. "So I called

Nyomi Malek and Brayson Bailey. Told them what we knew. I had to FAX over everything we'd gathered. An hour later there were reports online about two fiery crashes on the Interstate. When we saw the Bugatti, we were on the move. We knew it was you because you left in that car. We had to grab full containment of those crime scenes."

Joker was tired, but he said, "I pursued, caught up with them, and exchanged gunfire. The driver, the shooter, and Tithi… fucking Tithi, man."

Nina sat back in her seat. "Oh, Little Miss Aconite lives."

Joker wasn't sure he'd heard her right. "What?"

Nina nodded. "Lucky her. Lucky you. She's in the hospital in a medically induced coma from her injuries. She was badly burned but she wiggled free."

"I'll be damned."

CHAPTER FOUR

The Twin Towers
Chicago, ILL

Joker led the three-car caravan straight to the Twin Towers. Once there he was laser-focused on what he needed to do. He called Leah and Casci into the penthouse apartment office and closed the door. His fractured ribs were killing him.

"I need youz to fly to New York," he told them as he used his phone to schedule them a private flight out via charter jet. "I'm giving you the keys and the combo to the safe I have stashed at the Manhattan loft."

"You bought her a loft?" Casci asked sarcastically. "You never bought me a loft, David," she attempted to humor him.

Joker shook his head. "The loft belongs to EIE, Inc. She just thought she owned something. Also, remove her jewelry. There's a big amount of it. The loft is mine. I'm keepin' it. I just need y'all to go and bring all the cash and jewels back."

The two women nodded.

"Guess we'll sleep on the plane, Cash," Leah stated as she went to shower and get ready inside of her own apartment. "C'mon, girl. Make the arrangements, Daddy. I'll be back for the keys and directions there when I pack."

Both women exited the office.

"Nina!" he called out.

She was in the kitchen making a pot of coffee. "Breach, Ceasar… Bibleman."

The three mercenaries entered the kitchen.

"Do me a favor," she requested. "Pull something out the freezer and I'll whip it up. Chicken, shrimp, steak- doesn't matter. Put it under lukewarm water in the sink to thaw out."

"We got it," Ceasar told her.

Ceasar was a hardened Irishman. A former infantry solider in the U.S. Army. He'd also been a Blackwater mercenary who'd pocketed huge sums of money in America's secret wars to take oil fields in Kuwait and to assassinate various political leaders who the U.S. government wished to keep from seizing power. Joker had known Ceasar since their basic training days.

"The boss is back callin' for you in the office," Breach told her as he opened up the long rectangular deep freezer.

"I'm goin', I'm goin'," Nina replied, using a paper towel to dry her hands.

Breach was a tall, icy blue-eyed former U.S. Marine sniper and infantryman. He'd also been employed by Blackwater following his third tour in the Afghan War. Joker had been proud to have him assist his unit back then. Joker Red had been a Ranger but before the Rangers could go into Kabul, the Marines were called.

"Can you cook?" Breach asked Ceasar.

"Better than your mother," Ceasar told him.

"She said she'd do it, so let's just lay some stuff out. This fucker has elk."

"Yum," Breach said, taking the wrapped packages of elk steaks and jumbo shrimps which he placed into the sink. He ran the water on luke-warm to thaw the meat.

Nina entered Joker's office and he immediately said, "We got somebody on Tithi?"

"The FBI does," Nina mentioned.

"FBI," he repeated.

"Yeah, we need to find out everything," Nina added.

Joker had a grimace on his face as he tried to get up from his seat. "The CIA is interested," he observed.

"The fuckin' President is interested," she emphasized. "Because of the Albanian Mafia's ties to the Kremlin there is reason to be concerned. Their sex trafficking of Ukrainian children and women is an extremely lucrative market. Then the wave of mass shootings...."

He looked at her. "What about the mass shootings?"

"Law enforcement deaths this year have increased to fifty-three last I checked," Nina said as she stretched out on the sofa. "Our director pointed out the massive numbers of guns bein' confiscated off the streets. More and more we are tracing Russian-made weapons bein' in the hands of shooters and criminals. Many in the intelligence and law enforcement community think the Russians are behind the flood of weapons being introduced into American society. And many of those guns are Chinese and Hungarian-made but we know that they still came from Russia who trades with those countries."

Joker had a disbelieving smirk on his face. "Did Vladimir Putin tell y'all, 'I have given the Albanian Mafia a million guns to smuggle into America through the Mexican cartels and other Russian and Albanian smuggling routes?'" And why? So, he can sit back and laugh as all of these guns get into the wrong hands... mass shootings occur and police get hit up like them two who just got ambushed up Connecticut?"

Nina looked over at him. "I don't think the Russian President was quite so forthcoming. It's more complex than that."

"Remember the crack-cocaine explosion of the eighties and nineties?" He inquired.

She nodded. "Uh huh."

He stood up. "Same thing we got now, only it's a 'gun explosion' of the two-thousand twenties. Historical facts I'm sure you know about how the CIA was involved in drug trafficking with the South American and Mexican cartels. Specifically, the Nicaraguan Contras. Cocaine that ended up in the hands of Freeway Ricky Ross and distributed in southern California. First, crack was used to deliberately poison and addict the Black and Latino minorities so that President Reagan could fund his mufuckin' Central American War against the Sandinista Government - - a Russian ally."

"I can't disagree with that." She yawned and turned onto her side. "So, you think that the U.S. government - - the CIA - - is flooding its own communities *SOSAFROMSCARFACE* with all these guns on the streets today?"

"You ever read Lou Garden Price's book?" he asked, removing his jacket shirt.

She watched him. "No."

He took off his T-shirt and she eyed him more closely. She was curious about the through-and-through wound he had.

"Well...oww!!" He gasped and grunted as he removed the bandages on his chest. *Even wounded Joker looked so damned good,* she thought. "He expounded on the CIA drug trafficking pretty good. Anyhow, the way that the author crafted that story painted a horrifying but true account of what the American government is capable of."

She had to get up to help him walk back to his master bedroom because he was wincing with pain. "You mean with the guns."

He nodded as he sat down on his enormous bed. "Nina...President Reagan, Oliver North. The DEA and the muscle of your agency were instrumental–hands on–in narcotics trafficking in billions of dollars per year, for profit, of pure coke. That coke was turned to crack and it killed what Black and Latino America *coulda* been. They poisoned us to fund a crooked war in Nicaragua and El Salvador. That's what the public was fed anyway. Then the profits of that deliberate poisoning were used to fund all the new prisons being built. The criminal justice system boomed with profits... Now that the radioactive crack cloud has settled and the nation has more empty cell space... here comes another 'infusion of poison' upon poor people."

"The guns are the poison," she said.

"Exactly," he told her as he reached back and ripped off the bandage attached there. "The Oxycontin and Percocet opioid epidemic wasn't enough."

"Why?" Nina wanted to understand more about his interesting views.

He grimaced as she sat next to him and examined his wounds with her hands.

"First of all," he carried on. "They only start calling it an 'epidemic' when them crackers were affected. Back in the day when Blue Magic and China White heroin dominated Harlem, Chicago, and Detroit and whatnot, no one ever even heard that word *epidemic*. Why? Cuz niggas was hooked and dyin'! When the opioid crisis came they invented a miracle drug to bring them white boys and girls back from the dead when they OD'd. Only white people matter, dig? Word up."

"Naloxone."

"That's it," Joker said. "That wasn't it though. Once the President declared it a public health crisis, that opened up the doors for all those white mufuckaz doin' crime not to go to prison for drug-related crimes. The whites went to rehab while most niggas went to the fuckin' pen. But our greedy fuckin' government grows and thrives when the crime rates skyrocket. Look at these scumbag vultures: Oz, Fetterman, Biden, Mastriano, Harris – all these blood suckin' vultures politicizing crime in the hood. All the attack ads about shootings got niggas in it when most mass shootings involve white mufuckaz. This is all racist white propaganda bullshit they wanna use to refill the prisons. While the whole-time guns are ending up in the hood like nothin'.""

"Okay, Malcom X," she said finally. "You are in worse shape than I thought. Your ribs are mangled. The bruising and swelling is insane. I can see the pain in your face each time you try to move and breathe. And this wound could easily get infected. You may need surgery for the ribs before they puncture a vital organ - - like the lungs. And we need to see if that round you took broke anything or damaged anything we need to worry about."

Nina was so close to him that he could feel her breath on his chest as she cleaned the wounds and left them open. Joker asked her to help him bathe. She ran a bubble bath with hot water and left him alone as he soaked.

When he came out of the bathroom Joker was freshly shaved and feeling better. Nina returned a little later with a large tray that carried a plate of delicious-looking food.

"Breach and Ceasar did most of the cooking," she told him. "I fried the elk and made a gravy."

Besides the scrumptious elk, there was brown rice and vegetables. Joker was famished. She ate next to him. Casci and Leah returned to eat with them. But they left for the airport soon after.

Breach and Ceasar entered the bedroom carrying two bottled alcoholic beverages.

"We wanted to ask before opening," Breach stated as he held up a champagne bottle. "I saw several of these in the refrigerator: the Armand de Brignac."

"Ace of Spades," Joker said. "I don't care. Crack that shit. Whatchu got, Cease?"

"D'usse," he answered. "This is Jay-Z's cognac, right?"

Joker gave his tray to Breach. "Hey, Nina?"

"Yeah," she answered.

"See if you can find me a coupla Percocet in that medicine chest Uzenna nem got in there," he requested as he laid down. While she went in the bathroom he looked at Breach and Ceasar. "You two and Bible take it down for a coupla hours. Youse all gonna need the shuteye."

"We got it, boss," Breach said.

"Don't ask to open anything around here again, though," he ordered. "Just open it, son."

Ceasar and Breach left the room.

Nina came back with two 30mg Percocet pills. He took them with a beer nearby to wash them down.

She bandaged him up as best as she could. She also wrapped his mid-section up with gauze and Ace bandage. "I'm really worried about your health, Joker."

"C'mere," he urged her.

She shook her head. "I don't think so."

Joker caught her by her wrist and pulled her down next to him. "I'm not gonna bite. We just gonna sleep."

Nina took off her black jacket and shoes. She had double M9 Berettas holstered to her shoulders. She took the holster off and kept the weapons underneath the pillows. Then, turning her back to him, she laid down. He draped his left arm over her and easily curled around her slender stomach to pull her into him, spoon-style.

"I wish I could fuck you right now, Nina," he whispered against her left ear. "I been dreamin' about this chocolate body you got a thousand times since I've known you. That CIA badge you got means power to me and I love power."

She was grinning from ear to ear. "You are so smooth. Even with broken ribs and a bullet ripped through you."

She turned to face him for a minute. Then she eased into what became one of the most sweetest – if not thee sweetest – kisses she had ever had. Careful not to lean down onto his injured chest she savored the passionate way he embraced her, squeezed her ass, and moaned into her mouth.

"I like you, too," she stated, licking her own lips sexily. "And I want you. I want you to do what you dream of to me. Your polyamorous lifestyle I don't think I can do… but in a strange way, whenever I see you or think of you, it makes me wanna fuck."

"Oh, really?" he said more than asked.

"Sleep for now, okay?" She responded. "And then we are going to see a doctor."

He relented. "Damn… I'm so glad we got that out."

"Sleep, David Hodges."

They fell asleep, but this forbidden sex life of his… plus the fact that he was so pretty and rugged at the same time lit a fire inside of her flat belly. Nina had also seen that big lumber between his legs that Joker called 'the beast.' She snuggled closer to him and dreamed dreams of him she wished she shouldn't have.

CHAPTER FIVE

The Twin Towers
"Joker Leaves"

Nina woke up and moved her ass back into the throbbing heat of Joker's huge dick which had her pussy on fire all throughout her dreams. Even through her black tack gear pants, she had felt his monstrous manhood. It had to be 10 to 11 inches in length and at least the girth or circumference of her wrist and it even had a curve in it like a crescent or banana. She knew because she'd seen it clearly when she got up to pee. *He has a G-spot stroker.* She'd thought as half of it was hard as hell and poking up past his waistband to his belly button. She'd had to struggle to keep her hands to herself but what she had done was take off her pants prior to rejoining him after she'd peed. Then she placed her warm body back into the spoon position with her firm, but soft ass and pussy locked up against that beastly dick and balls he had.

She moved backwards again but didn't feel anything. Suddenly, she was sitting up wide awake with both M9's in her hands. She figured that Joker was either in the bathroom or out front with his men. So, she went into the bathroom to check and he wasn't there. She took a shower and walked out wrapped in a large yellow beach towel.

She searched through the dresser drawers and located clean panties. In fact, Nina found brand new panties with the tags still on them.

"Five hundred-dollar panties?" She murmured in surprise as she removed the tag from the soft red silk undergarment. "My God!"

She put them on and found a sports bra that fit her as well. She twirled in front of the mirror on top of the dresser on tippy toes so she could get a good look at her ass in the $500 Victoria's Secret panties and bra. She got dressed in her tack gear and boots and brushed out her shoulder-length hair. She put it into a ponytail, checked her face out in the mirror, holstered her weapons, and exited the room.

Breach and Ceasar were both dressed and ready to leave as well.

"Where's the boss?" Nina inquired, heading into the kitchen.

"Him and Bible left for the airport an hour ago," Breach informed her, pointing to the marble countertop that separated the living room from the kitchen. "He left you a text in that burner."

She picked up the burner phone and scanned the text message he'd left behind:

I have to disappear for a few to mend, think, train, and recharge. I'm trusting you to send me an alert if/when Tithi wakes up. I will seek medical attention.

The CIA agent felt kind of let down but she could understand because of the traumatic events that had been unleashed on his head. She bid Breach and Ceasar farewell and exited the penthouse.

Nina was on the next flight to Washington D.C. to do some regrouping of her own.

CHAPTER SIX

Ghostman & Honey B
Winthrop Harbor, ILL
The Albanian "NJË"

In Winthrop Harbor:

"WHAT? Still alive? How?" Ghostman's deep voice boomed inside of the living room as he stood in front of the fireplace facing his woman – Beatrice Lourdes Mendes-Diaz aka Honey B- and their new circle of sinister associates.

Honey B was nervous now. She normally had ice water running through her veins. Not now. This was something they had tried their best to plan for and be prepared to guard against in the event that their plan failed to assassinate Joker Red.

Honey B was the 24-year-old half Mexicana, half Puerto Rican wife of Steven "Ghostman" Adams. At one point, about two years prior, she had been the mistress of "El Verdugo" (The Executioner). Alberto Huerta Moreno had been the number one assassin and smuggler for the Juarez Cartel. He'd been a one-man killing machine for 14 years for his bosses and rumored to have assassinated 30 men and women during that time. Joker Red's rogue mercenary squad, EIE Inc., took out El Verdugo and his associates during a bloody operation backed by Chicago Mafia Boss Frank Braga.

She had a video recording of Ghostman committing the act of murder on a young girl. He could have killed her but he was so infatuated with Honey B that he'd allowed himself to be persuaded by her to conspire against Joker Red and the massive crystal meth empire he had built.

Honey B, a former high-end stripper, had had a daughter with El Verdugo who she had sent to a relative out of fear that Ghostman would do something to the child in order to force Honey B to relinquish the murder video. That was what she'd had in the back of her mind. What Ghostman had known when EIE had first kidnapped her as they were hunting down El Verdugo was that he had met a woman who had been degraded and underestimated for way too long. When Honey B had been his captive he should have just killed her. But once he'd started fucking her... he couldn't stop. She wasn't just a super bad "nine" she was a bonafide dime like a bitch Drake, Chris Brown, or A$AP Rocky would jump out the Phantom with at a Summer Jam concert.

Honey B had more than that though. She was a *bruja*. A witch that was cunning, evil, sweet, and knew how to use every cell in her body when it came to sexing a man, the half Mexican, half-Puerto Rican babe did more than fuck and suck a dick which 95% of women in the world think was okay. Honey B used her powers of seduction in and out of the bedroom. She cast a spell on Ghostman and accepted him as a bloodthirsty monster like no one else could or would. She knew he was a sick, twisted, serial killer who preyed on young unsuspecting girls. Frankly, Honey B had a cold heart too. She looked at her husband as a monster and the girls he hunted as meat.

Monsters need to eat, she often told herself when he'd return home with no explanation of where he'd been for 24 hours. She'd learned to recognize when he would return from a kill. A feast. He would end up grabbing Honey B and ravishing her.

"How old was she?" Honey B would ask after he'd kiss and suck wetly on her neck and lick her ears like she loved him to do while he was balls deep inside of her. "Was she white, Latina, Morena?"

"Chinese," he'd say. "She was nineteen…worked at Starbucks. She had small perky breasts. Slim with a little round bubble butt… Pretty face, eyes were coffee brown like that Starbucks she served… Her peach was bald…she tasted very good. She loved having me massage her back and eat her from the back."

"She has a cute little asshole?"

Honey B knew that shit got Ghostman going like a locomotive.

"Oh man, yes…yeah that little pucker was like a tiny belly button."

Ghostman told Honey B everything. Like a parishioner emptying his heart out to a priest to ease the crushing weight of sin to his soul in confession.

When she successfully persuaded him to let her lead the grand conspiracy to overthrow Joker for his crystal meth empire, Ghostman had carefully and methodically thought it through. Honey B had extreme *bruja* powers over him but he was no dummy either. He knew that if they were to be found out that there would be hell to pay.

"Baby, listen and listen real good," Ghostman had told her the previous year, even before she was pregnant with his son. "That nigga Joker Red is no ordinary nigga. He got the fucking U.S. Department of Defense… the goddamn CIA… and FBI on speed dial. No fuckin' nigga ever took or put together a whole fuckin' clan of former military personnel and done what he has done. Most of us are rogue soldiers. Dishonorable discharges, did some time in the Brig, probably shot, or even killed some fuckers in the war we never shoulda killed. But Joker was well-liked…by a lot and I mean a lot of soldiers. He was a leader and a warrior."

"Okay…so…?" Honey B had replied. "What's this? Are we backin' out or…?"

He had sighed. "Naw. I ain't said that. I'm just saying… we better be damned sure that your connections are ready for war, with a well-equipped, well-trained, rogue army of ferocious killers, snipers, bomb makers, and close-quarter combat soldiers who make really good money. Do you know how much cash that nigga's company just got on a bank loan?"

She'd shook her head. "You never told me."

"Seventy-five million dollars," he'd emphasized to her. "This mufucka is in so tight wit Don Frank... I don't know how da fuck he pulled it off but seventy-five million dollars on top of the millions he already got stashed. EIE is pullin' in twenty million each month from Meth Alley. He gives away duffle bags and suitcases filled with cash to the cops, TSA agents, CIA – even the fuckin' little kids all around the Twin Towers neighborhood get fifty-dollar bills to look out for danger, strange cars in the area, they take pictures of each car and person for him and text it to him. We cannot be half-cocked going in after the EIE empire. That's all I'm saying. If there are any mistakes in this war that nigga is comin' for our heads."

Honey B had taken all that into consideration when she'd assembled some of El Verdugo's most powerful underworld connections and she even chose to bring on board some of his formidable enemies.

The Tijuana Cartel sent three women to meet with Honey B after she'd convinced its bosses that she had a solid plan to move millions of dollars of their merchandise in Chicago and the infamous "Meth Alley" which stretched across the midwestern corridor. The three women sent to represent the Tijuana Cartel were Helena, Laila, and Nobi Jaramillo, the beautiful daughters and niece of Mexican drug lord Jose Pablo Juan Jaramillo.

The Gulf Cartel sent their best smugglers and assassins to investigate Honey B's proposition: Nico, Aurelio, Juan, and Kiko were sworn enemies of the late El Verdugo who'd assassinated two high-ranking members of the Gulf Cartel several years ago. When Ghostman was certain that the Gulf Cartel had no bad feelings towards her he'd let them proceed.

Then there was the Albanian goddess Valoria. She was tall for a woman. Standing 5'11" long shiny raven hair, slender, apple-sized breasts, thick eyebrows which helped to accentuate her silvery cat-like eyes. She was someone every man – and even 50% of women – really had to look at when walking towards her and past her. She just looked so good even though she was 39. That was prime age for women anyway.

She was from Durres, Albania. A resort city on the Adriatic Sea shores which was nestled between Tirane to the North and Elbasan to the Southeast. She spoke with an authoritative Eastern European accent yet she still had a sensuality about her that attracted Ghostman.

Honey B was an evil-minded witch but when it came to Valoria there was no comparison. Monsters were attracted to other monsters but Valoria was an alpha beast. Even Interpol had her on their radar, suspecting her of international sex trafficking and murder. There were rumors about her and the hundreds of ruthless Albanian Mafia at her disposal.

Ghostman would learn, as would everyone else, that the rumors about Valoria were not only scary but true…

"I thought you sent a female on the inside to fuck and feed the nigga some poison," Ghostman said, still breathing fire and anger over the acute failure. "How'd you fuck dat up?"

Honey B was upset because Ghostman was scolding her in front of their entire upper echelon unit in the organization: Nobi, Leila, Helena, Nico, Aurelio, Juan, Kiko, and Valoria – the head of NJË, the Albanian Mafia name which means "THE ONE" in Albanian.

"I didn't fuck anything up." Honey B snapped back at him. "We kidnapped Tithi's entire family, you showed her the torture video, we gave her the aconite plant poison…and it all somehow went to shit from there. Oh, and by the way, that bitch is still alive, too."

Ghostman laughed cynically. "Ain't this a bitch! Where is she?"

"Coma. The FBI is there with her," she stated. "Don't even think about silencing her."

Ghostman shrugged. "Bitch gotta die."

Honey B shook her head. "Bad idea. We still holding her family alive."

Ghostman nodded.

Honey B told him, "What if we told Joker where they were? It's a war move. Right now, he's in a blind rage. He's gonna hit us really, really hard. By giving up the family he'll put two and two together and figure out that Tithi was acting under extreme duress, not betrayal."

"Well, in that case, we'll send him the video, too," Ghostman said, agreeing with his wife.

She nodded.

"Smart thinking," Valoria stated. "He'll still know that he was betrayed but not by one of his wives."

"And Tithi was no ordinary wife," Ghostman sighed as he pulled out his cell phone and accessed the video where he had tortured Tithi's mother as she hung by the garage ceiling piping in chains. Next to her was Tithi's rich father and her younger brother. They'd all been badly whipped and electrocuted. But they were alive. Ghostman sent the video to Joker Red's encrypted cell phone.

"It's sent with a text on where he could go to free them."

"You face is disguised in there?" Valoria asked almost in a rhetorical tone.

Ghostman looked at her. "Didn't get all I have by bein' dumb, Valoria."

"Of course not."

CHAPTER SEVEN

Meanwhile, Joker was walking out of the doctor's office where he'd received some much-needed treatment for his three broken ribs and his gunshot wound. Dr. Felix Aroscoe had him seen earlier in the morning at Clark County General Hospital for MRIs to be taken of his injuries as well as x-rays. Joker was told he needed emergency surgery due to one of his ribs being too far pushed into his chest. Dr. Aroscoe was afraid that the broken rib could puncture his lungs which was what Nina had been wary of.

Also, he did have some bullet fragments lodged in his back that needed removing. Joker started up the 2022 Volkswagen Jetta he'd rented from the airport then he checked the text messages he'd received. When he saw the torture video of Tithi's parents he figured out almost instantly that Tithi had not acted out of malice but out of fear for the lives of her mother, brother, and father. He saw the location of where her family was being kept, locked up inside of an abandoned building in West Garfield Park.

He made a phone call to Breach.

"Breach," he answered.

"Red," Joker told him. "Y'all still in Chi-Town?"

"We here at your penthouse," Breach said. He told someone in the background. "It's the boss."

"Red! What's what?" Ceasar said.

"I'm 3,000 miles away," Joker informed them. "I'm sendin' you a video and other text info I got from… I believe it's Ghostman. Maybe Albanian mobsters. It's a torture video of a disguised torturer. Can't even tell his skin color or hear his voice so… look. It's Tithi's family. They're setting 'em free. Go get 'em outta there for me."

"Maybe it's a trap," Breach stated.

"Could be but I have my doubts," Joker told him. "Gather some troops up, you're in charge of the mission. I'll let Nina Overstreet know so you don't get any interference on this thing. It's connected to the highway thing so the FBI will want to umbrella it in with all of that. Once y'all pick 'em up turn 'em over to Nyomi Malek and Brayson Bailey."

They hung up and Joker relayed all the information over to Nina.

ON IT, was all she texted back.

He also sent her the information about his need for emergency surgery. Although he had Bible with him in Las Vegas, he told her, that he'd greatly hope that when he came out of the O.R. that she would have some time on her hands to help him recover.

Send address, time, etc. She texted back. *Can't promise anything except to do my best.*

Joker picked up Bible from the MGM Grand where they had two luxury suites on the 20th floor with a fabulous view of Sin City for miles. Joker pulled up outside of the West side entrance of the hotel where Bible stood waiting with a Louis Vuitton carry-on case.

"Bible," Joker greeted him as the enormous man nearly had to squeeze his way into the front passenger seat. "Durin' the surgery I want you to wait in the hospital parking lot for Stockton Rentals to bring us our car. When they do –"

"Bible confused," he admitted in his deep voice. "We have car. Bible fit."

"We're gettin' a bigger ride, B," Joker admonished. "And you are a size fifteen tryna wear size twelve sneakers, duke. If you call that fit maybe we need to find you a shrink. I already ordered a black Suburban. You know I'm the one who'll need the room after the surgery."

His good friend nodded. "Bible now understands."

They did some sightseeing down the infamous Las Vegas strip for a while before heading to the hospital. When they arrived Joker Red noticed that Bible was quiet.

"Why you so quiet?"

Bible shook his head. "Bible knew Ghostman was trouble… but woman he love has mark of the Beast. Jesus cast out demons by name in Holy Book. You know why?"

Joker left the car running so the air conditioning was still blowing. "You mean why Jesus called "them" by name?"

"They were once angels," Bible told Joker. "Jesus defeated them in heaven before when the Beast, Satan, rose up and tried to overthrow Jesus who is God in heaven. Anytime Bible have contact with Honey B… he only sees Beast eyes and…"

Joker sat deep in thought. "And what, B?"

"It was Eve who influenced Adam," Bible continued. "And many scholars have debated what Eve actually influence him with. What power did she have over Adam to even be able to influence him when the Lord made man the ruler over the woman, animals, and the earth. She used sex."

Joker stared at Bible. "I'm with you. I believe it."

Bible made sure he knew exactly where Joker was going to be inside of the hospital during and after his surgery before returning to the parking lot to wait on delivery of the Suburban. Joker was given a clipboard by the nurse where he had to fill out some documents. He handed them back in and looked at his cell phone. Uzenna, Iani, and all of his other women wanted to hear from him so he wrote out a text urging them to lie low and not leave Florida at this time. He also said he was healing just fine and needed time.

He was prepared for surgery and met with his surgeon Doctor Alan Saberi.

"You were a solider," the thin, white, gray-haired man smiled as he shook his hand.

"Still am," Joker acknowledged.

"We'll get you fixed up," the doctor promised. "We appreciate your service, where'd you serve?"

"Kandahar, Libya, Syria..." Joker answered as a Latina anesthesiologist placed a face mask over Joker's face. "It'll prolly be easier to list where I haven't fought."

The doctor nodded and walked off.

"Hey cutie, this is oxygen only," she told him. "Your eyes are amazing by the way."

Joker Red smiled at the beautiful red-haired Chicana. She was most likely in her late twenties, early thirties, with full lips, fair skin, and a provocative curvy figure. As he laid back on the gurney, several other medical personnel bustled and fussed around him. He was hooked up to heart and respiratory monitors.

"The gas sickens you, so the doctors ordered a sedative," the Latina girl told him. She injected a needle into the IV already in his arms.

"What's your name? Becky G?" he asked, comparing her with the gorgeous pop artist.

"You're funny, too" she giggled. "I am not Becky G but thanks for the big compliment. Your top came off and you got every nurse, technician, and female assistant in here finding an excuse to look."

He was put to sleep feeling good. The sedative had done its job.

CHAPTER EIGHT

Joker and Bible
Las Vegas, NV
Nina Arrives

The surgery was a success. The doctor was able to save all three busted ribs by resetting them and he also removed the fragmented bullet from Joker's back, shoulder, and chest would where it was a through-and-through shot.

"You wanna know what I think?" The surgeon said to Joker when he came to inside of his room. He showed Joker the bullet fragments just as Nina Overstreet appeared.

"There she is," Joker said, greeting her in a groggy voice. "Dr. Saberi, meet Ms. Nina Overstreet."

The doctor shook her hand. She was dressed in a black leather skirt and a sleeveless red satin top by Gucci. She really came in killing it. She had the blazing red and gold Gucci purse, Gucci glasses, and no high heels but some black and red Gucci sneakers. Every nurse and female medical assistant on the surgery team had hopes of slipping Joker their phone number, Instagram, Facebook, or something. But when Nina came through looking like the sweet goddess of chocolate gold and diamonds, their hopes were dashed.

The Latina anesthesiologist entered the room with several other assistants as the doctor spoke.

"We have another surgery to do," the doctor said from where he sat holding a plastic bag with the .223 bullet fragments in it. "I was just telling Mr. Green here what I thought. He said he was shot while conducting drills. Normally AR-15 ammo doesn't frag unless it strikes a bone or it could ricochet and hit you. I'm glad you came in because you never know what materials manufacturers are mixing into their ammo: lead, copper, tin, and God knows what other toxic alloys."

"May we have that?" Nina requested the fragments.

"Hospital policy is strict about this sort of thing," the doctor told her. "We have to contact the Clark County Sheriff's Office and -"

"I'll take it to them." She showed him her CIA credentials and he paused for a moment. Nina stated, "He's a soldier, I'm his handler. National Security Act, doctor."

He handed it to her. "There you go. No problem. Wow, CIA here, huh?"

The doctor exited.

"They're keepin' me 'til tomorrow," he informed Nina as he had trouble keeping his eyes open.

"That's okay," Nina replied as she took a moment to hug him and stroke his wavy hair and the side of his face. "I can tell you need to sleep."

"It's the sedative," the Latina anesthesiologist said as she monitored his vitals on the screen.

"I'm sorry, what's your name again?" Joker inquired in a whisper.

"Not Becky G," she replied with a small laugh. "I'm Ida. And nobody could believe a CIA agent would walk up in here."

Nina gave the woman a half smile.

Bible came in and took a seat on the side of the second bed in the room. "The Lord told me to tell you somethin'," Bible said as he laid out across the bed and turned on the TV.

"What?" Joker looked his way.
"To get that ass up," Bible stated.
Joker fell asleep on him.
Nina smiled and settled in at Joker's side.

CHAPTER NINE

The MGM Grand
Las Vegas, NV

A week later Joker, Bible, and Nina were returning from a 5-mile run at 4:20 AM to their hotel at MGM Grand when they headed straight to their gym to work out. Joker was almost back to 100% but not quite there yet. That didn't stop him from trying.

They did some weightlifting and MMA training for nearly two hours before quitting and returning to their suites for showers. The three of them fell asleep until noon. Joker was called down to the Manager's Office where a FedEx courier was waiting for him.

"Hodges?" the FedEx man inquired as he held a Plexiglass clipboard in his hand. He was of Mexican descent and he stood next to the office entrance with a stack of packages on a hard plastic cart.

"This from Chicago?" Joker asked, showing the courier his ID.

The courier nodded. "Yes, sir."

Joker signed for the delivery. He pushed the cart onto the elevator and went back to the suite he shared with Nina. He opened up the box and was happy that everything had arrived intact. Nina entered the living room area of the multi-room suite and observed Joker removing what had to be millions - - perhaps three million - - of dollars in $100 bills from some of the boxes and placing the cash inside of a black trunk. Each package of cash he picked up had been professionally stacked and vacuum-packed by a special machine. Most likely a restaurant-quality food-packing device.

"What's this for?" She asked as Bible entered.

"You'll see," he promised. "Leah had emptied out a stash I had in Tithi's loft and sent it to me."

Nina, who wore a lovely bathing suit the color of bright red, black, and white striped patterns, tied a sheer red sarong around her lithe waist. "That's a lot to FedEx…"

He removed brand-new weapons: handguns, silencers, rifles, tactical gear, and a box of grenades. He thoroughly inspected each weapon before placing it into the trunk. He even stopped to assemble and then disassembled the sniper rifle that was included inside one of the boxes.

"Night vision goggles… infrared binoculars too huh?" She commented. "Are we goin' squirrel hunting?"

"Now you know me better than that," Joker told her slowly. That sinister smile of his was back. "I don't go pickin' on the small or the weak. I want the biggest and baddest monster there is. Right, Bible?"

"David and Goliath," Bible replied, following Joker's lead on putting together a long-range .22 rifle and breaking it down again.

Nina chuckled.

"Let's get packed up," Joker told her. "We goin' on a lil road trip. Leah sent me some info we need to act on."

～

"Rose Rice Donohue"
The Desert Pines

WHILE LAS VEGAS WAS MOSTLY KNOWN FOR ITS MAJESTIC HOTELS, casinos, mega-large nightclubs, and party-til-you-drop atmosphere, there was much more to it than that. There were hotels where a room could cost $10K per night and there were hotels where a trick could take a hooker for $20 per hour. Some liked that high-end "get high" for $1000 on great champagne while others craved a poor man's "get-high" for only $10. Sometimes that $10 could buy a hit of crystal meth that would help keep the buyer high for hours and, at other times, that same $10 could cop a bag of fentanyl-laced heroin that would put the buyer in the morgue where death claims him or her forever.

Nina drove the luxury Suburban to one of the more run-down hotels in Las Vegas called The Desert Pines Motel. Bible and Joker, both wearing black tactical uniforms, waited for Nina to park before they scoped out the activity at the hotel. There were prostitutes hanging out on the upstairs deck of the motel. There were more than fifteen hookers, transvestites, homosexual boys, and tricks coming in and out of rooms on the ground level. *A den of sin*, Nina observed.

"Thirty on top, forty on the bottom," Joker said, counting the rooms. "Nina, this is no DOD or CIA mission…"

Nina was listening, "Okay so why are we here?"

"Rose Rice Donohue," Joker stated as he pulled up her photo on his encrypted telephone. "Surely you've heard of this pretty little blond-haired blue-eyed white girl from all the media attention she got for being missing."

"I've seen her," Nina acknowledged.

Joker sent Nina the email he'd been sent by Leah. He interpreted it for her in shorthand terms. "Basically, what she's saying is 12-year-old Rose ran away from home in Washington, D.C. and was lured to Las Vegas by another girl who Rose thought was close to her age on the KIK app. Turns out that this girl who baited her is also bein' trafficked by a Las Vegas pimp but she's his bottom bitch. Rose turns tricks out of this motel unless ordered to do otherwise by the pimp or the bottom bitch."

"This girl is endangered and missing," Nina finally spoke, sounding somewhat baffled. "If Leah knows, how doesn't the police know?"

Joker shook his head. "We ain't into callin' the cops. We ain't into lockin' mufuckaz up. We either goin' in and takin' out the entire cancer or we ain't' doin' nothin'. Plus Leah… well, she randomly searches for missin' people using her hackin' abilities. She don't need a warrant to do what she do. She knew I was out here, so she sent this case to me. She knows I despise sex traffickers, so we locked in."

"Yeah," she said as Joker looked around using the binoculars. "Why do you hate sex traffickers so much? You never talk ab-"

Joker dropped the binoculars and opened the door suddenly. "Keep it runnin', baby! Bible!"

Nina had no idea what Joker had seen but it was obvious that something caught his eye because he was out of the vehicle in a flash. Both he and Bible pulled their identical black demon masks up over their faces and advanced toward the hotel.

"I just saw the bottom bitch enter a room," Joker informed Bible.

"Copy dat," Bible said as they approached.

Room 127 had loud rap music coming from it. There was a double window but the curtains were drawn. Knowing they had to act fast and hit hard, Joker looked at the massive "Bishop Warrior" standing before him.

"Bible, door," Joker ordered.

Bible's face seemed to smile at first and then snarl as he, almost effortlessly, stepped back and delivered a single kick to the door with the sole of his right field boot. The door's upper hinges busted clear off the door frame as it crashed in. Bible followed through with his menacing .45 Glock raised.

"SHIT!" Nina cursed inside of the SUV when she saw Bible smash the door in like the *Incredible Hulk*! She removed her own M9 Beretta, cocked it, took it off safety, and put the SUV in drive. She moved closer to the room.

Back inside of the motel room Bible observed a nude, heavyset, Black man thrusting his bone into a white girl from the back while she held onto the pillow and the sheets for dear life on top of one of the two beds. Joker covered them while Bible covered a fully dressed raven-haired female - - a Chicana - - sitting on the foot of the second bed smoking a cigarette. She was reaching inside her black Hermes bag.

"Mm-mm!" Bible shook his head. "I'll kill you first. Take hand slowly out!!" His voice boomed.

She immediately complied. "Don't shoot!"

Bible checked the bathroom. It had another female inside. "Come out! Now!"

She was a young Black girl, wet from just having taken a shower. She came out of the bathroom wrapped in a pink towel.

"Sit!" Bible indicated with his weapon.

She sat next to the "bottom bitch."

Joker was pistol-whipping the Black trick. "Get yo dumb ass outta here!!" Joker yelled at him. "That girl's a fuckin' twelve-year-old!!"

The trick had blood trickling down the left side of his face from a cut Joker had caused next to his eye. He was afraid, his flaccid dick swinging, as Joker beat on him. A second later the frightened Black man was snatching on his slacks and shirt before hightailing it out of the room.

Bible was emptying the "bottom bitch's" Hermés bag onto the dresser top. She had a nice but deadly .25 caliber pistol in there. He removed the clip and discharged the bullet that was in the chamber. He gave her all of her things back – including the gun.

Joker looked at the white girl. She was about four feet eleven, 100 pounds, with red hair and blue eyes. She was strikingly beautiful but Joker knew right away that this was the target missing girl Rose Rice Donohue.

CHAPTER TEN

The Rescued Girls
En Route to Death Valley

"Cuff 'em, bring 'em!" Joker ordered Bible.

Bible saw a summer dress crumpled up on the floor and threw it at the young Black girl.

"On!" Bible barked at the startled Black teen.

Seconds later he had the bottom bitch cuffed with flex cuffs as well as the Black girl. While they were doing that there was a commotion outside. Joker had seen that the 12-year-old missing girl was whacked out on some kind of drug that had her smiling as she looked at him. Whatever it was she'd been given had her thrusting her right ring and middle fingers inside of herself as though she was itching her womb.

"Fuck you on?" Joker said as he wrapped the young girl in a blanket, scooped her up onto his left shoulder, and followed Bible outside.

There in the parking lot, Nina was embroiled in a hand-to-hand death match with a man who had her outweighed by at least 70 pounds. He was white, had a lot of tattoos, and had dark hair. Thankfully, she had brought the Suburban closer to the room. Now it was easier to secure the three females inside of the truck quicker so he could assist Nina with her fight.

Dozens of the motel's residents – mostly Black, Latino, and 'White trash' females who were welfare victims—poured out of their rooms to see the action. Joker secured his missing target in the vehicle with her seat belt on as did Bible with the other girls.

By now Nina had the man subdued with a powerful leg lock around his head and neck while placing his arm into a position where she could easily have broken it. He was gargling as if he had mouthwash caught up in his throat. Then he lost consciousness.

Bible came over, cuffed the man with flex-cuffs, and checked his pulse. "He's alive."

"Let's move," Joker snapped as he hopped into the sleek new Chevy Suburban.

"Y'all ain't no fuckin' cops!" The girl known as the 'bottom bitch' commented from the rear of the vehicle.

Nina, breathing hard, her nose bleeding, drove away from the hotel. Joker sat in the back with the three girls. First, he looked at the Black girl.

"How old are you, mama?" he asked her.

"Eighteen," she lied.

"I'm not a cop," Joker said as Bible handed him his laptop.

"What are you?" She asked indignantly. She was cute, a brown/light brown color. Her eyes were a light brown as well. She was certainly underaged. She was bigger than Rose Rice and a little heavier, too.

"Let's start with your name," Joker diverted the question. "Your real name and where you're from."

"Fuck you," she cursed him and looked out the window she was seated next to.

Joker nodded and produced a small stack of $100 bills. "Fuck this, too?" He queried, cutting the flex-cuffs off of her hands.

She accepted the money. "Kalani Muhammad. I'll be fourteen in two months."

The bottom bitch sucked her teeth. "They'll kill you for talkin' to these fuckin' people, Kalani."

Joker entered the teen's name and age into the database for missing and exploited children.

"From Jersey?" Joker asked her. "This you?"

Kalani nodded. "East Orange."

Joker looked at the bottom bitch. "How old are you, Miss Toughy?"

"You won't get me to talk," she said. "You stepped on the wrong people's toes, asshole. We belong to the Albanians."

"Really," Joker said more than asked.

"That Vato you attacked out there is called Nuri," she informed him. "He's the Vegas Mob muscle for his brother Drak or Mad Wolf from New York."

"New York's a long way from here," Nina interjected while driving out of Vegas.

"Don't matter. Where you think they brought Kalani from?" The bottom bitch shot back. "There's two hundred girls they got out here and that's just the ones I know. I only manage fifteen."

Joker was going to have Nina pull over and drop the bottom bitch off the side of the road before they headed out to Death Valley California. But he changed his mind. He took the girl's Hermés purse and found her ID card.

"Ariel Montoya," Joker entered her name into the database as he said it out loud. Moments later, he nodded. "You've been missin' since you were twelve. Now you're nineteen. You know what you've been put through by these vicious cock suckin' Albanian pigs…so why put these twelve and thirteen-year-olds through it?"

"You can't judge my shoes, *ese*," she said in the accent of an East LA Mexicana or Chicana homegirl. "Not til' you lived in 'em."

Joker moved back to her row of seats and removed the flex cuffs. "You right, shorty. I'm not judgin' you. I'm showin' you. Youse an adult. Any second these streets are gonna swallow you up, peel the flesh off your body, and fuckin' coyotes and foxes will bury your bones. That how you wanna go? At twenty? Twenty-one at the most?"

He turned the televisions on in the headrests.

"We headed to the Death Valley strip?" Nina inquired.

"Affirmative." Joker eased back in his seat and handed Ariel a stack of $100 bills. "You, Kalani, and Rose are all safe with us. I would just let you go but…we need to talk more. At least return home to show ya folks your face. That you're alive."

"I'm not goin' back home," Ariel said, vehemently shaking her head. "All I did was get beat on by my mom and father. I hated catholic school, catholic church, and catholic confession. I was forced to pray, wear ugly dresses…and when I refused I'd get beaten. I'm not going back."

"Me neither," Kalani said.

"Why?" He probed, looking at Kalani.

She never said why.

Later, during their drive to Death Valley, when Kalani had earbuds in – watching a movie – Ariel told Joker, "Kalani has a mother who cares for her, a mother in their house in New Jersey. Two of Kalani's brothers started molesting her at ages five, six, and seven. When she was caught in the bed naked with her brother, her mother saw red and beat her so badly that she ran away. She was blamed for her debauchery. The mother never thought that she had been raped by her own brothers ever since she'd been very young."

"Aight." Joker went back up front to check on Rose. She was sleeping it off, whatever "it" was.

"How long before we get to the airfield?" He asked Nina.

"Sixty minutes."

CHAPTER ELEVEN

The Death Valley Cabin
11:00 PM
Death Valley California

EIE owned a cabin in Death Valley where they came to train when necessary. The cabin itself had been upgraded and renovated. It only had three bedrooms, but it was two stories high, built with more than 20,000 feet of high-grade cedar. It sat on six acres of land with several huge Rottweilers, a horse stable, and a barn. On the edges of the property were a rock-choked ravine and a lot of desert weeds.

Joker employed a Mexican family to live on an acre for the property, the house, and the animals. The family lived in trailers at the end of the land limits…

Joker carried Rose Rice Donohue inside of the house. Since it was 11:00 PM, a cold had blown in over the desert, so Joker and Bible set fires in all three fireplaces of the cabin, and they got the girls comfortable. Nina put Rose in bed, tucked away tightly in one of the guest rooms. Kalani was placed in the other bed in the same room.

"You go ahead in the master bedroom, Ariel." Nina directed her.

"Who are you?" Ariel asked her.

Nina pulled her credentials and badge out of her rear back pocket. Ariel read it and her mouth opened to talk but she couldn't.

"Speak your mind," Nina urged her.

"The way you took Nuri out," she said. "I never seen a female do anything like you did. I knew you were someone special."

"You need sleep," Nina told her. "We'll talk."

Kelani took off her shoes and slipped into the bed.

Joker sent for one of the EIE airplanes to come pick them up. When he was done on the telephone he sat on the bear skin rug-covered sofa. "The plane will be here tomorrow," Joker informed Nina and Bible.

Bible laid out an air mattress, sheet, and blanket. He found a good pillow, took off his jacket and boots, and laid down.

"Please tell me we're not going to war against these Albanians on the West Coast," she said.

He laid down his head in her lap and replied, "Nah. We got a war to handle back east first. Anybody human, especially Black, should despise those who make slaves of other people. You asked me earlier why I hate sex traffickers so much. That's why. Because I know our history as Blacks. I especially hate those who force women and children into sexual slavery. I saw it in Al-Qaeda, ISIL, and I *hate* it."

Bible, who was nearly asleep on the floor in front of the fireplace, said, "*This charge I commit unto thee, son Timothy, according to the prophecies which went before on thee, that thou by them mightiest war a good warfare.* First Timothy Chapter One verse Eighteen."

"Whattaya mean, B?" She inquired.

Bible yawned tiredly. "Brother Timothy was being met with challenge in the advancement of the gospel of Christ. Apostle Paul told him to hold firm. Similarly, we see our cause as one having challenges… and we are soldiers who dare to wage war against those who prey on the weak. Our war is a good warfare."

One of the girls screamed. Bible immediately jumped up with his guns in hand. He heard the crying and was followed into the room by Joker and Nina to where Rose Rice Donahue was.

"Y'all go 'head," Bible said to Joker and Nina.

"What, you have a nightmare, little one?" He asked her after turning the lamp on. Joker put another two logs on the fire.

Nina went into the kitchen to cook some food.

"Where am I?" Rose asked, no longer high on whatever she'd been high on.

"California," Bible said as he put some pillows behind her so she could sit back more comfortably. "My name is Eustace Reed but everyone calls me Bibleman or Bible. I'm a United States Army soldier. So is he. His name is Joker Red. He's our boss."

"You have to take me back!" She begged. "I need to go back. They'll kill my family."

"Look. C'mere." Bible reached out for her and held her tiny hand in his humongous one. "Don't worry about any of that. We'll protect you and your family okay?"

She nodded, still afraid. Joker found it interesting how adults-grown men even- trembled at the sight of Bible. He was so big, as though he were some sort of freak of nature. But most young children loved him. He was a gentle, protective, giant with them.

"We took you away from bad men," Joker said as he sat on the chair next to her bedside which Bible sat on. "How 'bout we get you back home to your mommy and daddy?"

She nodded. "Do you have my shots?"

Joker frowned. "Shots?"

"Medication?" Bible mentioned.

Nina came back into the room and put the large bed tray down on Rose Rice's right. She had made hot chocolate, a delicious vegetable and beef (canned) soup, cheese cubes, and crackers. Nina had heard Rose speak about her shots and paused.

"Check her for track marks," Nina suggested.

Bible inspected her inner arms and saw evidence of heroin use. "Great God Almighty…she's addicted to junk. What're we gonna do when she withdraws in a few hours? We got nothin' to give her til we can get her to rehab."

"I got somethin',' Ariel said as she entered the room.

"What?" Joker wanted to know.

The Latina entered the room, close to the bed, and reached into her pocket. She pulled out several baggies of heroin which were bundled up inside of another Ziploc plastic bag. She gave them to Joker Red.

"The Albanian had you givin' this to her?" Joker questioned her.

She nodded, meekly. "To half of them…the ones hard to control. Rose was scared so they started her on heroin. The only way she'd get her shot was if she'd work."

"You the one they use to lure other young girls online, huh?" Nina probed.

"Am I in trouble?" Ariel asked her.

"I'll be honest with you," Nina said. "You should be but you're a victim too. A victim these bastards used to enslave dozens of other children for sex. If the police or FBI were to arrest you… some would charge you as an accomplice because you know what you're doin'. They wouldn't care you're brown, a Mexican."

"Chicana."

"Whatever. A Chicana or Chicano is a Mexican born in America," Nina stated. "Point is you are as Black as any of us and these racist fucks won't have no sympathy calling you a pimp like they did to Ghislane Maxwell. We know you was caged and raped but them crackers won't care. You got Rose on the KIK app to come to Vegas?"

Ariel nodded. "To run away… what're y'all gonna do with me?"

"You gonna help the government," Nina revealed to her. "You have a new job now. Those doses you've been giving her?"

Ariel nodded. "Yeah?"

"Cut them in half," Nina advised. "In the morning or afternoon, our airplane will be here. We'll figure it all out, but Las Vegas is over for you. Don't get any funny ideas either, sweetheart."

"Whattaya mean? I'm not," Ariel declared.

Nina used her cellphone to text Ariel's pimp – Nuri – an incendiary message. "That Albanian is aware now that you set that raid up at the motel. I texted him already so… they're lookin' for you, Miss Montoya. If you fuck us or run, you're dead."

"Why would you do that?" Ariel shouted.

Nina stood in front of Ariel. "I'm CIA. We always think several steps ahead. If this was a fuckin' chess game I took away one of your most powerful plays. You play on our side or nothin'. If you want trust, you're gonna have to earn it around here."

Ariel spun around and returned to her bed.

Joker followed Nina out. "That was cold," he said.

"Mr. Bible?"

"Yes, Miss Rose," he answered.

"Can you stay with me in here please?" She asked.

"You bet, child." He grabbed his blankets and pillows from the living room and laid them out in front of the fireplace in Rose's room. "Good night."

"Good night," she returned. She finished off the food and sat the tray off to the right of the large bed.

This time there were no nightmares.

CHAPTER TWELVE

Young Army
Custer, South Dakota

The C-40 Clipper landed at the clandestine EIE paramilitary base in Custer, South Dakota. They were only there to do a temporary stopover and pick up "Young Army" who'd been living and training there for months. For the most part, they were eighteen "young bucks" from out of Fort Greene Bed-Stuy area of Brooklyn who Joker had snatched up to invest in. All of them were related to Joker as either cousins or nephews (and one butch female which was his second cousin).

"C'mon, y'all niggas, let's move!" Joker shouted as he stepped off of the luxury jet onto the tarmac.

Young Army members Smoke, Rome, and Brook were Joker's sister's sons. Natasha Catherine Hodges was his sister. The rest of the Crew was Jimmie 2 Tymes, Mojo, Blood Money, Steetlyfe, Big Crip, Badman, Hop, Tip Toe, Grim, Boom, Budda Clips, Blue, Cocaine, Crime, and Rampage (the butch female second cousin).

"They told me you were over here whinin' like a bitch, too," Joker said to Rampage. "Can't even handle a Glock. Talkin' bout yo name Rampage."

She scrounged her face up like Martin Lawrence. "You need to shoot whoever said that lie. A Glock? Them shits is like water guns to me, cuz. Fuck outta here."

Joker hugged her and smiled. "You slimmed up good, too. I see they got rid of that gut you had."

She smiled back and got on the plane.

Shortly, the plane was back in the sky with its engines screaming.

~

West Palm Beach

THE PREVIOUS WINTER, JOKER RED HAD BECOME SO DISTRUSTFUL OF people that he had worked with Nina and Lieutenant Sampson Gates to establish what he called his Central Intelligence Network or CIN. It was located inside of an office complex where an entire four-story building was leased to them in West Palm Beach.

Not far from CIN, Uzenna and the others had found a spectacular 23,893 square-foot Mediterranean-style super villa with a hefty 8.5-million-dollar price tag. Initially, when Joker had first seen it, he thought it was going to be hell to guard. But Lieutenant Gates had brought in a professional security team made up of former military and law enforcement personnel. There was an army of them there at the vast estate, patrolling it with armored SUVs around the clock. Each of the Joker's wives had security with them everywhere they went.

When Joker Red and the others landed at a nearby private airfield they were loaded into various Cadillac and Range Rover SUVs and driven to the beautiful palace. Nina was not with them. She had stayed with the plane so she could be flown to Washington and then she had to be in Chicago.

"Daddy!" Uzenna gushed as she burst out the front doors of the mansion.

They stood in the center of the marble and granite driveway

hugging and kissing. One by one his lovely wives came running out to greet him with love and affection. All of them were there: Uzenna aka Butterfly, Coral aka White China, Brittani, Ashley, Eden, Leah, Valerie, and Uzenna's older sister, Iani.

"Hello, sweeties!" Blond bombshell Valerie was saying to Rose, Kalani, and Ariel. "And who are these cuties?"

Rose ignored her as did Kalani as they both grabbed onto Bible's hands. Joker directed Young Army to empty the gear and suitcases from the vehicles.

"Bible," Joker said. "Go with the nannies to get Rose, Kalani, and Ariel settled into their rooms. Y'all get bathed up and eat dinner. The FBI, Rose's mom, and dad will be here to pick her up. Hopefully, they'll stay quiet about her rescue… I'd hate to hear the Albanians got to her over a Tweet."

They entered the foyer of the palatial home.

Uzenna instructed one of the armed security to escort the Young Army to their cottage. She knew Joker didn't want the rowdy young men in the main house because they were just too much.

"I need to shower," Joker said. "And see my children. Here, baby. Put this up."

Uzenna took the bag containing the cash Leah had Fed Ex'd him. "This is heavy," she exclaimed.

"Anybody gonna show me the way around this monster fuckin' castle?" He asked as he lustfully eyed each of his beautiful wives.

"C'mon, Daddy," Ashley quipped as she grabbed ahold of his hand. "To the master bedroom. Let's get you showered first. Babies second."

Ashley was normally more laid back and quiet. Ever since their daughter – Sonja Dee Hodges – had been born, Ashley had begun to blossom out of her shell a little more. Joker had known very early on with these amazing women that they'd been traumatized for years. Way before he'd come along to liberate them from the iron grip the Mafia had had on them, and as such, it would probably take years to peel back the hardened layers on each of them.

Before their deaths, Ashley had probably been more like Louise, Melodie, Diane, and Julia. They had been loving towards him but still not with that 100% relaxation… They all loved and respected what they had with him but it still took some time to truly know him and 'warm up' to him.

What he now saw with Ashley's forwardness was a 100% comfortability that wasn't there six months ago. She was more confident and he loved it. Eden led him down the east wing corridor to an elevator that the eight of them rode up to the next level and it opened to the most luxurious master bedroom he'd ever seen.

"Damn," he whispered. "Rich people shit."

Eden and Iani giggled as they sat him down in the sitting area and helped him out of his combat boots.

Minutes later he was laid back inside of the sunk-in "Scarface Bathtub" soaking in a bubble bath. The bathtub was so large it looked like a small swimming pool.

"Wow," he murmured. "This that El Chapo, Puff Daddy shit! That's right. I'm ridin' wit P. Diddy, homie."

Several of his wives saw where he'd been shot and started to cry. Eden, Ashley, and Uzenna started first. Then their tears caused all the rest to burst into sobs. It was clear how close they'd come to losing him.

"Now, now, c'mon now," Joker said soothingly. "Y'all get undressed, grab some beer, and catch me up. I'm a warrior. It's another scare outta many. I love y'all too. Now let's laugh, not cry."

They all joined him in the tub.

CHAPTER THIRTEEN

(AKA) "The Palace"
West Palm Beach, FL

Uzenna and Leah sat at Joker's sides while they and all of his wives lazed in the steamy Jasmine and lemon-scented bubble bath. Each of them relaxed while sipping from glasses of a $5000 bottle of Courvoisier XO.

"You said she's addicted – the little white girl?" Iani asked.

Joker nodded. "I think the Albanians fucked her up for life. Bible said she's having nightmares. Real screamin' horror shit."

Uzenna ran her hands up and down his back as he spoke. "What are we gonna do about the other two? Kalani and Ariel? I like Kalani."

"Nina's takin' her and placin' her with someone she trusts," Joker informed them. "She needs to be debriefed on what she knows about the Albanians and whatever intelligence is gathered, it'll be passed on to the FBI and other law enforcement I guess. That ain't our job. Kalani can't be returned home. Unless she has a grandmother or somethin'. She was bein' raped by her own older brothers ever since she was five. One day when she was caught in a sex act with her brother, her mother beat her half to death. They're in North Jersey so she ran

75

away to NYC. She was seen there on the streets by an Albanian Mob Boss called 'Drak' aka Mad Wolf according to Ariel. His people scooped her and hundreds of others up from New York and trafficked her to Las Vegas."

Coral used a big, soft, soapy sponge to wash one leg and foot while she spoke. "Leah, you located the white girl how?" She clipped his toenails while they spoke.

"Just pokin' around," Leah replied with a shrug. "She was all over the news so…"

"Being an online sleuth," the beautiful dark-haired Ashley elaborated.

"But everyone knew she was missing," Valerie mentioned. "How'd -?"

Leah explained a little more. "I hacked into the police's database and found out later what the National Center for Missing and Exploited Children had. I saw that she had a secret KIK account from an email she had at her school. And a female friend was sending her dozens of texts a day. And these girls were sizzling online lovers. Anyway, Ariel was being used to lure these lost types, daddy issues, mental health issues – girls who were vulnerable, out to Las Vegas or New York."

"Into straight traps," Joker said as Leah leaned in and suckled his ear and neck. "You've become truly amazing with your computer skills. You should be proud of yourself, baby."

"We're all proud of you, Leah," Uzenna told her.

"We saved three young girls," Joker said, hugging Leah, embracing her and pulling her onto his lap. He stared into the 5-foot 6-inch, 140-pound, beauty's big blue eyes. He stroked her blond hair with the black dye streaks she'd had styled into it. "Youse a superstar, Mommie. You also led us into a hornet's nest."

"That's bad?"

Uzenna chuckled.

So, did Joker. "Usually, if you open up a hornet's nest it's very bad… But youse onto somethin'. I have every reason to believe that the Albanian Mafia is the mastermind behind those bombings that killed four of my wives and four of my fuckin' kids. Plus, my comrades, Monk, Black N9NE --"

"Don't Daddy," Leah said, leaning up to face him with her pretty, pink-tipped breasts pointing at his chest. "Don't get riled up. Those were our sisters… our comrades… and our children's three sisters and one brother who died in the blasts. I know it's an open sore still…but let's focus on justice."

"Our kind of justice," Brittani remarked as she slowly stepped out of the tub. As she walked away towards the shower and sink area her tattooed buttocks jiggled like a California earthquake in a China shop. Joker's eyes were all on it… how the bathtub bubbles clung to her skin and slowly dripped down her shapely body. And he could see her bald pussy lips from behind.

"The Central Intelligence Network is the Twin Towers War Room on steroids," Joker said. "Each of you now have jobs at the CIN under Leah here."

"No more Chicago?" Eden wanted to know.

He shook his head. "No. Chicago's done. For my wives and kids that is. The Twin Towers, other investments, our strip clubs, the meth labs, the whole Midwest empire are still rockin'. They tried to use Tithi to poison me."

The girls were listening with profound attention.

"No good fucking bitch!" Uzenna said angrily.

"Her family came from across seas to visit her," he explained. "They snatched Tithi's people up and threatened to murder them. They told her, probably to shoot me in my sleep but Tithi… she ain't a thug. She ain't got no felony in her heart like y'all."

"But she poisoned you," Uzenna reminded him.

He shook his head. "Tried to. Poison is a female's murder weapon. In her mind, it was a merciful way to kill…"

"You talkin' like…" Iani started, "like you forgivin' it."

"You readin' me wrong," he told her. "I could never forgive a woman who chose to kill me over her family. I'm just explaining and sayin' I could understand why. She didn't do it for money or jealousy or anger. Leah flew to New York and Fed Ex'd me millions from a safe I had in that Manhattan loft."

"I wish I could live there!" Leah stated with a delightful smile.

Joker continued. "The South Dakota airbase and CIN are interconnected, and we have backing by the CIA. It's a secret, secret, top secret affair we got and y'all ain't allowed to talk about it. Hey, Leah… Honey B & Ghostman? Target them. We gave them what they believe are encrypted cell phones. See if they still have them. If not, start elsewhere. Their Wi-Fi, hack into their internet searches, emails, new cell phones, etc. So youse know – I have a mole in their house."

"Apolina?" Uzenna guessed. "The Panamanian girl?"

"*Exactamente*," he said in Spanish. "If or when Tithi comes out of a medically induced coma the FBI will grill her while Nina observes."

"It's a bigger picture to all this, huh?" Uzenna asked curiously as she waded around the sudsy tub. She wanted to suck he husband's big dick and get fucked. Bad.

He tilted his head to the left, not forgetting Uzenna's past transgression when she had called herself leaving him and taking their son – Baby Joker #1 – with her. However, he made himself *pause* because she had done more than enough to redeem herself. She had even accepted a severe sexual punishment where she was whipped so hard on her deliciously round ass cheeks that she'd bled. But the pleasure derived from the wild spanking and fist-fucking bonanza that day had changed her. She was more submissive towards him now and more obedient. She masturbated almost daily as she thought about him dominating her, spanking her bare ass cheeks, and fucking her like she was his personal slut.

"Of course, there's a bigger picture," he finally answered. "Them fuckin' bastards tried to have me poisoned. Then as I chased 'em with my four-million-dollar car, I killed the driver and shooter of the car Tithi was in. I was tryna kill her but learned later that she was burned badly and was in a coma. And from nowhere, a fuckin' blue Dodge Charger came up on my blindside. That's how I was shot, lost control of my shit, and nearly ate the fuckin' dirt. If it wasn't a bigger picture I'd be in Chicago in a mansion across the street from Ghostman with the owner's bodies thrown in the basement. I'd have a fifty-millimeter sniper rifle ready to blow his fuckin' noodles out. Goddamn right, it's a bigger picture."

He paused as he got out of the tub.

Brittani gave him a large black and gold towel. "You're a king, Daddy. If any of my family were abducted… I'd never betray you. Them bastards can die slow."

"None of us would," Uzenna added.

Joker nodded. "I'll tell you this through… if it came down to one of my kids and me then Imma dead mufucka. Y'all hear me? Sell me out if it comes to one of my babies."

The women nodded.

"That's what the beefed-up security's all about," he said to them as he applied baby oil to his skin that smelled like Blue Nile Muslim oil. "I need long hours out of y'all at CIN even after we neutralize Ghostman and Honey B. The intel we have so far from Apolina is that they are joining forces with Mexican cartel members and the Albanians. The CIA and FBI are extremely interested in them all now that I was nearly killed. See, we think strips clubs, meth, millions… the CIA is more focused on the Albanian/Mexican cartel connections because of the potential for bombs, nuclear materials like plutonium, or for terrorists to be smuggled into America across the U.S.- Mexico border."

Everyone got out of the bathtub and dried off. The women put bathrobes on and exited to their own rooms to get ready for bed. Uzenna had to show Joker where all of his underwear, socks, T-shirts, wife beaters, sweats, and other clothing were. Everything was inside of a massive closet one had to see to believe.

"What da fuck?" He said amazed. "Wow."

There was a huge circular restaurant-quality black leather cushioned sitting area for the "footwear closet." There were sturdy glass shelves that the wives had decorated with shoes he never even knew he had. The sneaker shelves had all of the new and vintage Jordans.

"This the whole Jordan collection?" He asked her. "Are these real Retro Four Jordans?"

Uzenna smiled proudly. "Daddy, is that even a question? Mogul style. Suge Knight at Death Row Records in its prime. You a fuckin' mogul. Jordans, Nikes, Adidas, NB's, all the Tims, you love Balenciaga, Armani, Gucci, Louis V, man Fuhgeddaboudit. You got it all. New suits, ties, and… you wanna see your watch and jewelry display?"

He smiled as he nodded. "Yeah. Show me."

She pointed at two doors next to a floor-to-ceiling mirror. He opened them and inside was a glass display case. Uzenna pressed a button and the glass slid aside automatically.

"You heard of Pristine Jewelers, right?" She asked as she pulled out a diamond watch.

"Goddamn- hell yeah," He said but hesitated to take it. "Gucci Mane, Gucci Mane's wife, Puff Daddy – they got 'em. Baby… this a million-dollar watch!"

She put it on him. "We know you don't like the flash. But we know you a Black Prime Minister like one of them Arabs or somethin' in Dubai."

"You spent a million dollars on a watch," he stated in disbelief.

"You mad?"

He laughed and kissed her. "Yeah and no."

She sucked her teeth. "I sure hope you not because we went watch crazy. We bought you all the Richard Mille watches. C'mere."

She had on black lacy boy shorts with red hearts on them. Her small t-shirt was black as well with the words "LA DOÑA" emblazoned across it in pink. The t-shirt did nothing to conceal her fantastic booty cheeks. She knew what she was doing, too. She was aware that those particular boy shorts really rode up high in the crack so whenever she'd bend over or reached her hand up for something, he could see how snug the boy shorts cupped her juicy pussy.

They walked out of the closet after he put on new boxers, a black tank top, and blue New York Yankees sweatpants. He couldn't help but think how her pussy imprint looked like a baby's fist or something in those boy shorts. He was definitely thinking of fucking her…

There was a cell phone she picked up and showed him a code he had to punch in. When he did, a hidden door opened near the arching windows where there was a glass door leading out to the master bedroom balcony. He went over to the wall and pushed it inwards. Uzenna walked in through the other side and he followed her. He couldn't keep his eyes off her ass either. He needed some pussy so bad. He could've fucked Nina but... the time wasn't right.

Uzenna used another combination to open the door behind the hidden wall. "This is the vault," she said.

Nothing was remarkable about the room itself. It had plain white steel shelves inside along all three walls. A top-of-the-line money counter sat on an Oak table and paper money bands were inside separate plastic containers in $1000, $5000, $10,000, $20,000, $50,000, $100,000, and $1M denominations.

Money was neatly stacked on each shelf. He started at it and said, "This a lot of fuckin' cash. Meth Man Ace?"

She nodded. "Not directly from him. His girlfr- I mean his wives: Blanca, Bambina, Natalya, and Alejandra."

"We haveta stop courier cash," he said. "Meth Man is leery of bein' on camera so all that cash flowin' from Meth Alley has to be deposited into our bank account. We have no IRS fears. Plus the cash smells like dope. Airport K9's are gonna sniff his wives out."

Uzenna shrugged. "All that ain't my lane, Daddy. By the way, remember our orgy down here last month?"

"When we first checked the house out?" He inquired as they locked the room up and secured the wall. "We have a lot of orgies, babe... When I spanked you?"

Uzenna sighed. "Not when you spanked me in that glorious sex attack."

He laughed as they laid down on the Ultra king-sized bed's humongous blue velvet comforter. "You funny," he told her.

"It's freakish," she admitted. "But I swear, Daddy. Don't laugh. I need that type of sex so bad. I mean I came so hard and so much. I just crave it and need it. I even bought a whip and tried to hit my ass with it while on my stomach masturbating. I spank my pussy some too... I get so hot."

He looked at her. "For real? Baby, your ass had open wounds on it. It had blood."

She was nodding eagerly as he spoke. "Yes! Please yes! You just don't know I guess. It's what I need."

"Okay," he said, kissing her and reaching back to squeeze and swat her buttocks a couple of times. "That shit is hot anyway."

"Ooo, I need to tell you," she started and then stopped. "Nevamind."

"Girl, spit it out!" He prodded her.

"Leah, Eden, Coral, and me are pregnant," she gushed finally. "We wanted to tell you together."

"Whaaat?" He said, surprised. "That was left field! You serious, huh?"

She was slowly nodding. "I think it happened when you disciplined me. The raunchy passion you, Leah, Eden, and Coral was doin'. They want babies."

"And you don't?"

"At first I wanted to wait until our son was up and runnin' so he could help a little but I'm okay with it. I'm happy."

He held her to him.

"Me too, baby. Me too," he said. "But y'all don't have free lives right now. Not while Ghostman lives. Y'all can't do anything except be here or at CIN a mile away. There's a war goin' on and my enemies know my weakness is my wives and children."

"Okay," she accepted his orders. "We have everything we need here. We'll be fine."

They were both exhausted and finally fell asleep in each other's arms.

CHAPTER FOURTEEN

Joker woke up with the roosters and the earthworms. He washed his face and brushed his teeth before using the toilet, showering, etcetera, etcetera. It was barely 4:30 AM when he left Uzenna in the bed snoring lightly. He walked through the "Palace" and could only think of one word to describe it: sick. Absolutely sick. The place was one the Kardashians or a billionaire would own most definitely.

Ten bedrooms, ten full bathrooms, three partial bathrooms, an indoor swimming pool, and a full gym, it was 2-story, it had 7 garage bays, tennis courts, basketball courts, 8 to 10 feet high ceilings, a covered lanai, cabana, breakfast nook, a covered balcony, a fabulous back deck, outdoor swimming pool, a private lake, marina, and large wrought iron gates. At the lake end of the property were two cottages that were constructed for the help to live comfortably in. Both cottages contained a dozen two-bedroom apartments and every amenity a resident could possibly need while living there.

He visited each of his children's beds: First his son (King) with Romie who was now dead for her treacherous infidelity with A-Son. Next to King was his son with Uzenna – David Leon Hodges, Jr. aka Baby Joker I. In the next bed in the nursery was Bradford which was his son by Coral. Then there was Sonja, his and Ashley's lovely daughter. David Leon II slept next to her. David 2 (or "Baby Joker 2") was his and Leah's son. Eden and his daughter, Eve, was asleep in Eve's bed. Eve must not have been able to sleep without her mom last night, so Eden had curled up with her.

He looked at little Ivory Brown Hodges who was his daughter with Valerie. He took her thumb out of her mouth.

Then Iani and his daughter Rose were in the next bed asleep. And, last, there was his son with Brittani, David Leon 3. He looked back at Rose who was his tiny twin if he ever had a female version of himself.

"Daddy?"

He turned around at the doorway and saw Leah standing there in a long purple robe. He walked towards her. "Whatchu doin' up?" He whispered.

She grabbed ahold of his hand and led him down to the indoor swimming pool area where steam wafted off of the top of the water like it does from a hot cup of tea. Leah was smiling hack at him as they got naked and waded down the steps into the warm water. He sat on the fourth step and Leah wrapped her legs around his waist and back.

"You know how much you mean to me?" He asked as he placed several loving kisses all over her forehead, eyes, nose, and lips. "I mean do you?"

She nodded. "Yeah. You know how much you mean to me?" she emphasized.

"I believe I do," he said as she kissed him back. "Why you ain't tell me you pregnant?"

She gushed, all shy and pretty. "I was gonna but you was on the road healin' up and all after… Chicago."

They tongue-kissed like they hadn't seen each other for ages. Each devouring the other's mouth. He was sucking her tongue and lips as if he was trying to suck all of her sweet saliva away. She smelled very good and tasted even better. He knew one thing: his chocolate cucumber was so hard he felt like he could use his shit to win the World Series… With all home runs. The NY Yankees need the help!

She felt on his arm and chest muscles and how hard his abs felt. "Babe, each time you cum in me it won't stop leaking out for a day and a half. You should know Imma be pregnant. I can literally smell your cum still comin' out two or three days later."

He believed it. He smiled. "You like that?"

"No!" She laughed and kissed him again. "Yeah. I be havin' to switch panties cuz I'm a clean girl. Your sperms be taking my mind off my computer work cuz it gets all squishy between the lips."

"Speakin' of sperms." He sat her up on the edge of the swimming pool and loved how the blue night lights around them bathed her white skin and caused her blue eyes to darken to a shiny cobalt color. "I ain't had none in a minute! Feel how big and swollen my balls are. All the hair's gone, too, fresh, hard, and smooth how you like it."

"You ain't fuck Nina?" Leah inquired, suppressing jealousy.

He shook his head.

"She wants you," Leah stated, cupping his scrotum and stroking his monster. "Damn, I swear youse a foot long… God your balls are mad fat, Daddy, you ain't lyin'… mmm, not here."

"Why not?"

"Bible's up, one of the nannies could get up - c'mon!" She got up. "Grab the clothes, Daddy. I want you for myself. If any of the wives see us I have to share and with how horny I am...? No way!"

She led him out into the shower area and into one of the private rooms in the rear. Those rooms had massage tables with sofas, a fully stocked mini bar in each, digital televisions mounted inside of the walls, and a fancy electric heating unit to warm the room up. There were three such rooms. Leah led him into the last one and locked the door.

She turned on the television to access YouTube and when she did, she played her love song playlist starting with Whitney Houston's "You Give Good Love."

He laid her out on the sofa, kissing her face again, humping his huge beast into her slick labia without even aiming, the big shiny head, dripping with his own pre-ejaculate, had heat-seeking capabilities, and it kept threatening to thrust itself into her small wet orifice which was like a swimming pool down there.

"I love you, Leah," he whispered. "I'm in love with you, your loyalty, your intelligence, everything. This bangin' ass, these pretty titties, suckable toes, your face, how you smell… I can smell your horny pussy scent filling the room right now, baby. I fuckin' love it."

"Fuck me! Fill me up with it right now!" She demanded as the big head of his horse dick continued to plant its own version of squishy wet kisses on her other set of lips. "Stop teasin' me, Daddy. Push it in."

She was gyrating her full hips and ass upwards against him, trying to capture that big dick inside of her wet opening. Her clit was extended out from beneath its protective hood, rubbing up against his corona. Each time she pressed her clit up against his pre-cum covered monster dickhead, electric currents of pleasure shot all throughout her body, making her stomach tighten, and juice trickled out of her vaginal canal, down over her asshole.

"What the fuck you doin' wit that pretty ass pussy? You tryna sneak out a fuckin' orgasm?" He accused her as he snatched both of her hands up and pinned them above her head. He licked and wetly sucked on her neck. Water and perspiration on her skin. "You bein' sneaky?"

"No."

"Liar." He left hickeys everywhere. "They'll all know you were fucked and… sucked… and punished like the slutty little criminal you are. Now open them thick white thighs and let me at that filthy, pretty, slutty, dirty, white girl pussy. I said: open 'em up! Wider!"

His dirty talk turned her on way past ten. He sucked, bit on her nipples the way she liked on his way down. She moaned out her pleasure as he let her hands loose. She squeezed his head and pulled him back up to get more of his hot kisses. His kisses made her float on air.

He smelled all over her neck, her clean-shaven underarms which smelled like chlorine now from the swimming pool mixed faintly with her Dior perfume. He licked all over her smooth underarm areas which caused her to pull him more tightly to her. The erogenous zones in that taboo area combined with the pheromone glands there did something wicked to both of them.

"Oh my God, you make me feel so good!" She whined.

He grabbed both titties again and rubbed his face all in between them. He sucked on her rosé-colored nipples, hungrily biting on them and slavering his tongue all over them, loving them.

He wasted no more time. He was gonna taste that pinkness.

"Ooouuu!" She breathed and moaned slowly out as she masturbated her own breasts. "You gonna need that towel, Daddy. It's too wet… too much juice. Ooouu, Daddy, dry my pussy first… ohhh fuuuck! You so nasty…so nasty, God suck that coochie, baby! Put your nose deep in my pussyhole!"

She spread her legs wider until they looked like butterfly wings. He was up in that bald little mango, using his lips and tongue to taste and suck along each of her pulpy labial love lips until they were wet and glistening. She opened like a flower and his tongue followed her pussy cream down to her anus and she turned over onto her stomach without even asking. She knew how much he loved to eat ass. And it wasn't just the boost his ego got of seeing his name tattooed back there (on her left lower hamstring and bottom asscheek area on the left leg was "My King" and on her right leg, same area, was "Joker Red"). Sure, he loved all of that, but the man just loved to have his face planted in the female asshole and ass crack. He was profoundly into the clean musky scent of his women back there. He knew every crinkle around her little anus, and she got off on perching her pretty ass up and reaching back there to open it up for him.

"I smell your pussy cream all in your asshole, baby," he told her, slashing his tongue up through her warm crack, up then down, up then down, as if there was vanilla icing in that thing.

"That's that 'Leah Juice,' Daddy," she purred while pushing her stuff more firmly into his fine-ass face. She needed to cum so bad and if he kept swiping her from asshole to clit- how he was currently doing- and using his big fingers to flick her… she would surely burst into the flames of orgasm. "Keep pinching my clit, Daddy… damn! Keep lickin' my pussy and asshole like that! Like that – shit, Daddy! I love that fuckin' thick long tongue! Ohh, fuck, oh, fuck, oh, fuck, Joookeerrr, yes Daddy!! Mmmm, taste that?! You taste that extra Leah Juice, baby?! Oh fuck, shit, shit… soooo goooood. My pussy is bustin' all crazy. Clit all hard. Ooousogood!"

He slapped her ass and put his face up against her pussy to smell it once more. It was definitely the Leah Juice cum scent now. But Leah needed several orgasms to make her content. She turned over and pushed him back so she could taste him.

"Ohh, I can't take much of that," he cautioned as she wrapped her pink lips around the salty-sweet knob. "Mmm, Leah, take the beast and suck him real good. You love that big black dick, huh?"

"Mmm, I love to suck your big black dick. My dick. My beast. Mmm, ohm! Glrrb!" She sucked with loud raunchy slurping noises.

He closed his eyes and leaned his head back. Her head game was classic, superior, and dangerous because Leah was that badass white bitch who was always underrated. Like a Hollywood underdog chick who was clearly the best-looking and best actress but was never promoted right. Such as "Anya Taylor-Joy" (The New Mutants) versus Jennifer Lawrence. Anya is clearly the better actress and way better looking… That's Leah all day.

She looked up at him and spit all on and over his monster shaft to make sure it was slick enough. "Every time we about to do it I can never believe it'll fit. I get scared."

He got on top of her and guided him into her. "You can take him, baby. You can take him, baby. You can take the beast. I just can't slam your uterus to pieces because of our new baby. I gotta treat you care-fully- like a virgin."

Her pussy had already been turned to liquid gold by his licking, his fine looks, and dirty talk. "Yessss, put that big dick in me! Ooouuu, slower…God, yeah, it's stretching my little pussy, Daddy! My Black King, Daddy Joker Red Hodges! Take it now, Daddy! Make me your little white slut!"

He sunk it all in slow but deep. "Leah, Oh, Fuckin' Leah yeah! I'm in, I'm in. I don't wanna hurt him or her but I am in this white pussy!"

"Slow, you fine ass Black motherfucker! Slay this sweet white pussy slow. God, the beast is so HARD in me!"

They made love. Passionate, easy, slow love for the next forty minutes. She really enjoyed it when she rode on top of him with her beautiful titties pressed hard into his chest. He grabbed the globes of her ass as she rode that big monster, opening and closing them to increase the sensuality.

Then she turned over and busted that fat ass all the way open and laid her face flat against the soft leather sofa. Her love songs continued to play in the background. Trey Songz was back there killing it as Joker rubbed the head of his dick around her opening. He placed the head of his dick back into the rim of her little pussy and pushed. He glided his beast in and out and she had one orgasm after another as he swiveled his hips sexily, stretching her and stretching her.

"This the only dick for you," he whispered as he flattened her on the sofa. "You feel how that curve in my dick keeps hittin' that g-spot real good? It's touching it right now, huh?"

She was gasping as a puddle of her lust formed underneath her as proof of what he said. "Yes, Daddy! Yours is the only dick I'll ever need! Oh my God... I fuckin' squirted! I never squirted! What'd you do to me? I'm so wet! It splashed everywhere, Daddy! Oh fuck..."

"Nevermind all dat," he whispered as he sucked her ear and neck and smelled her breath and her hair. "Just know I got the beast- the master key to this body. This pussy. You. Look under you again!"

He put her on her knees but kept her convulsing pussy still wrapped around his pole. She looked down at the cushion at the wet mess she'd made. It looked like someone spilled a glassful of clear corn syrup there.

"See?" He said, placing his hand in her lusty juice puddle and showing it to her. "It's like I stuck my hand in the rain."

He sniffed his hand and felt the beast lurch. "You smell fantastic. I smell your scent and get harder."

He put her back onto her stomach and stroked himself in and out of her stirring that mango up as he did so he hit every wall and nerve-ending she had. He reached under her and toyed with her dripping wet clit. Soon he was sawing into her again and again and again. He was holding both of his arms under her as the lovemaking turned to fucking. But careful not to fuck too deep.

"Fuck my ass! You're hurting my pussy, now, Daddy," she whimpered. "I like it but the baby. Push that monster beast inside of my little asshole."

She reached back and opened up her ass cheeks. "Go ahead, Daddy. I been usin' a dildo and a butt plug on it. I can take it. I found out my ass is a second pussy. Please."

It was already plenty lube back there, so he placed the head of his dick up against her anus and pushed. She helped by relaxing and opening up. His dick plopped through as her sphincter gave way. He was able to push almost all the way into her and then he froze so that she could adjust to his size for a couple of minutes.

He kept his hand on her pussy as he started fucking her ass. After a few minutes he was fucking her asshole as if they'd been doing it for years. She was twirling it, whimpering loudly, throwing it back at him, begging for more.

"You love it, huh? You love to fuck, babe?" He asked. "I'm about to cum! Here it cums, Mommie. Oh shit. Oh, fuck yeah. I'm tryna hold this shit ooouuu, your asshole and pussy look so…oh my God, I smell your sexy scent baby! Damn, that ass smell so good!!"

His enormous chimpanzee balls tightened up more than ever and he buried the beast super deep down inside of her clutching bowels and relaxed his powerful body across her much smaller one. He pulled her wet hair and forced it to the left so that they could see each other, feel each other's breaths touch, her full lips beckoning him in for a final orgasmic sexual kiss as their sweaty bodies careened into their last act of the sweet moment.

"Fuck my little asshole, Daddy. Ohh, I love your big fuckin' beast in my navel, it's past my navel. It's too deep in there! Ooouuu!!! You're makin' me c-c-cuuummm… Leah Juice, Daddy! My fucking cunt's exploding Leah Juice while you fuck my ass!"

He licked her wet pink lips and short stroked her ass-lining slowly but he couldn't hold it back no longer. "Cuuuuummmmmiiiinnngggg,

Leah. Oh God, Leah, ohhh, ahh, Fuck! All in that sweet-white ass! Feels so good… smells so good…"

She twirled and swung that sweaty hot backside of hers around and around under him as what felt like a cupful of his warm liquid goo coated her insides with a magical heat. Feeling his warm seed pour into her sent goosebumps throughout her body. When they both calmed down he stayed inside of her, laying on her back, swaying left and right. Lost in the aftermath of a mind-blowing session of love and lust. Minutes later, they disengaged and cuddled on the sofa until sleep overtook them.

But from interval to interval, they would awake to kiss and whisper words of love all over again.

"Lemme up, bae," he said around 9:00 AM.

"Umm mm- you go…" she murmured.

He covered her with a giant beach towel and went to swim nude once more, washing away the physical remnants of the sex before drying, dressing, and returning to his master bedroom. He heard Uzenna in the bathroom. He poked his head in there.

"I was wondering where you were!" Uzenna said, surprised as she stepped out of the shower and stood in front of the mirror.

She had on an all-white terry cloth robe with a blue shower cap on. She removed the shower cap. He moved up behind her and ran his hands over her hips and buttocks. He was hard instantly. He opened a drawer up, found the Viagra, swallowed the blue pill, and smiled at his lovely young wife.

"Baby?" He murmured as he ridded her of the bathrobe.

"Hm?" She said as he left a trail of hot kisses across her neck and shoulders then pulled her into the bedroom. He laid her down on her stomach.

"I'm obsessin' and fetishizing right now," he said as he planted his face and nose up against her asshole. She smelled like an expensive body wash which he liked. "I need to eat and smell your asshole… mm… just hang on for the ride babe."

CHAPTER FIFTEEN

The Donohue Family Arrives
West Palm Beach, FL

Joker was down at the lake with all nine of his kids having a ball with them all by himself while Bible and Young Army were on the lake itself betting on jet ski races. Uzenna and the other mothers wanted to keep the children – most of them over a year old now – "socially distanced" from everyone that could possibly give them coronavirus, monkeypox, or RSV so Joker wore a face mask around them. So, did everyone else. Bible, Young Army, and others like them agreed to stay away from the kids entirely for seven days.

"Rose, come to Daddy, baby girl," Joker said to the beautiful little girl as she fell while chasing one of the cats that made the estate their home.

The little girl got back up onto her tiny bare feet and ran towards her father, falling again. This time at least she wasn't in the mud. Just the sand.

"Yo, mama said not to let y'all get sand in your hair and not to muddy up your clothes, and whatchu do?" He asked baby Rose as he picked her up. "You too, Miss Ivory Brown- bring yo little butt over here."

His daughter with Valerie came to him and reached her little arms up so he could pick her up. She had come outside with sandals on as had Rose. The mothers had insisted that the kids keep shoes on to protect their feet. As he looked at Ivory Brown Hodges the child was shirtless.

"Ivory- where's your shirt, Mommie?" He asked her.

Ivory looked at him with her shiny little face and pointed at Rose. "Rose shirt, Daddy!" Ivory said.

"Your mom gonna have a fit and you don't care, do you?" He asked her and she giggled. "I know you don't. Gimme kiss, honey."

She kissed his mask and he put her down.

"Give Daddy kisses, Rosie," he said to his baby with Iani. She kissed him where his mask was too.

He put Rose down and looked at the four puppies that were out there playing with the kids. A dozen highly trained murderous presa canario dogs were in the kennels and a breeding pair had produced a litter of pups. Four of them were given to the children. Joker walked over to one of the puppies and saw her with Ivory's ruined shirt in his mouth as he chewed and played with it.

"Ivory," Joker said, looking down at her. "You too damned young to be havin' your little tatas out in public."

"Who got their tatas out?" Uzenna asked with a smile on her face as she and the other sister-wives came out onto the sand-covered lakeside.

He looked at Valerie and said, "Valerie's crazy little *Girls Gone Wild* over there. Ivory!"

The kids were running around with puppies, two cats, bugging out, screaming all crazy.

The women laughed at Joker's humor at how Ivory had become a "Girls Gone Wild" like the racy videos they used to sell back in the early 2000s of college girls lifting their shirts up to show off their breasts to cameras.

"These kids are a muddy mess, J.R." Iani stated as she inspected

Rose's long, nicely styled hair. "She had pictures bein' taken tomorrow. That's why I ain't want her to get sand in her hair."

"You got me in trouble, Rosie," he blamed her.

"Daddy, the feds is here with the rescued Rose's family," Uzenna informed him.

"Maaan, shit!" he said. "I'm chillin' wit my babies and here come these bozos. Can't get a goddamn minute."

He walked over to the lake and waded in up to his knees to rinse off the sand between his bare toes and like small Mexican bulls all of his babies came wading out after him. The women helped him round them and the puppies up before they all drowned out there.

"That makes me concerned," he said as he put on his Gucci slippers and headed up the long winding path toward the main house. "We need a fence blocking all of this off in case any of them break free and run down here thinkin' they Michael Phelps. That goes for them pups, too."

"Who's Michael Phelps?" Eden asked as the girls laid towels out on the sand.

"The Olympic swimmer," Valerie replied. "Like Katie Ledecky."

In the living room, Joker Red entered and walked straight behind the bar saying, "Nobody's wearing face masks, so I'll speak from over here."

He pushed a box of medical-grade masks over the gleaming marble countertop of the long rectangular bar. He poured himself a cold mug of Heineken from the draft spout.

"I can't believe I have real draft beer where I live. Forget the mansion. Real Heineken draft. Can you believe it?" He smiled as every one of his five guests took a mask and put it on.

Present in the room were Nyomi Malek, Brayson Bailey, Zach and Faith Donohue, and Nina Overstreet. Joker called Bible over the walkie talkie and ordered him to come in the living room.

"These are Rose Rice's parents," Nyomi stated more than she introduced. "We've had multiple conversations with the case agent in D.C. where they are from, as well as with Mr. and Mrs. Donohue and there's a divide on what to do."

Joker's eyebrows raised as Bible quickly entered the living room with his shirt off. He looked like he had had just stepped off the stage at the World's Strongest Man contest. His small beady eyes scanned the room, landing on Joker Red.

"Praise the Lord," he said, panting. "Bible come fast."

"What's the divide on what to do?" Joker asked Nyomi. He looked at Bible. "These are Rose Rice's parents, B. Imma say now…ain't gon' be no divisions on nothin'."

"Well…" Brayson Bailey spoke up. "The FBI and other case agents on the task force assigned to locate Rose Rice unanimously believe that bringing her back to D.C. will put her life in danger. The Albanian Mafia will be looking to silence her as a witness."

"The Donohue's think they'll steer clear to avoid further implication of the suspects involved," Nyomi said as Nina went behind the bar to try that mug of ice-cold draft beer that Joker was drinking.

Joker hugged her briefly and moved out of her way. He sat on a counter behind the bar near the sink.

"Why D.C.?" Joker asked the Donohue's flat out.

"I work at a natural gas company as an engineer and my wife works for Microsoft," Zachary Donohue explained. "We have lucrative employment, a house, and -"

"You want a dead daughter?" Joker cut him short. "A decapitated wife?"

"No, I -" Zach stammered. "We can hire a security guard to escort her everywhere."

Joker came from around the bar. "The Albanian Mafia are animals from hell, Donohue. They'll splatter your mall cop's brains like a water balloon. Lemme tell you…no. Lemme enlighten you…"

He removed his shirt and pointed at the .223 through-and-through shot he'd suffered.

"This is courtesy of them scumbag Albanian mufuckaz, ya heard?" Joker had a stoic expression on his face. "As I was still healing from that wound and bein' thrown from my vehicle – well I actually chose to jump – I received an emergency assignment regarding Rose. The Albanians were usin' another sex trafficking victim to lure God knows how many girls into their stable. Your daughter was attracted to this four-teen-year-old girl who showered her with over ten thousand hours of phone calls and text messages. Bible here, my dearest comrade, brother, and friend, breached the hotel door and I witnessed a fat black monster layin' it to your daughter – unprotected. I pistol-beat him and let him escape with his life. Inside the room with Rose, was a young thirteen-year-old separate missing girl, and the fourteen-year-old who was the valuable key to one of many Albanian trafficking operations. Anyway, while Bible and I were readying the girls for transport, my friend and comrade Nina here had been outside in the vehicle. She was fighting like MMA underground with an Albanian pimp or muscle in Vegas for the real boss who's in New York. His name is 'Mad Wolf.' In my opinion, the girl goes to D.C., and the media gets a whiff of it, not only is she dead but so are both of you."

Joker drained the entire mug of beer and walked back around the bar to wash it out, dry it, and put it back where it belonged.

"Can we please see our little girl?" Faith asked.

Zach stood up. "God, Faith, what'll we do?"

"Look, man," Joker said to them. "Your daughter is decompressing and has a rehab nurse here with her twenty-four-seven. She's really become attached to Bible here who sleeps on the floor in their room."

Zach and Faith looked at Bible. The man himself at first glance was a Frankenstein, a monstrosity. His legs – tree trunks. His arms and torso – were herculean.

"R-rehab?" Faith repeated the word.

Bible cut in. "Albanian men evil. Use dope in the needle to turn Miss Rose Rice into a zombie."

Faith swallowed. "You mean she's a heroin addict?"

"Right on," Joker said. "It's not her fault. The old trick traffickers and pimps been usin' since the start of prostitution – to control her. That means she was resisting and fighting. So to control her they addicted her. When you get that diesel in yo veins… even a pretty lady like you'd be willin' to do the whole D.C. for a fix."

Faith cringed at Joker's cynical analogy.

Both Zach and Faith became quiet. Then Faith burst out sobbing and shaking with tears. It was all sinking in now. It wasn't only "abduction, rescue, freedom, case closed."

"So, you guys are cops? FBI?" The tall dark-haired Zach queried.

"Nooo," Joker answered.

"Well," Zach said, looking at Nina. "You had the monster who did this. Did you lock him away?"

"Hey!" Joker boomed, snapping Zach out of it. "Cool it. Like I said, Rose Rice is decompressing. Being treated for addiction. She's off heroin. We had to give her small doses to keep her from withdrawing too bad."

"You actually gave her heroin?" Faith asked.

"Ma'am," Joker stated, holding a halting hand up. "I had to treat young boys, girls, even captured ISIL and Al Qaeda soldiers who were addicted to Afghan heroin. You can't just drop them cold turkey. It could make them convulse, lose consciousness, hallucinate, even die. Your daughter is on a doctor-prescribed med called Suboxone right now. A synthetic opiate which helps block the urge to use heroin and even if she does, it won't have an effect."

"If you want her to be cared for as you…process it all, leave her here," Nyomi urged the two distraught parents. "Meanwhile stay silent about her whereabouts and go about life as usual knowing that your child is safe."

Zach looked at the opulence of the vast living room. *Who are these people?* He thought. "You're not cops, you're not FBI, who are you? Don't I have a right to know who I'm leaving my child with?"

Joker nodded. "I'm Joker Red. True name David Leon Hodges, U.S. Army Ranger, combat fighter, sniper, trained martial arts expert, owner of PMC company: EIE, Inc."

"PMC?" Faith asked.

"Private Military Corporation," Zachary answered for her. "They're commandos, sweetheart. We owe you thanks. For your service to the country and for saving our -"

His voice cracked with emotion and tears filled his eyes but he walked away. Faith followed him and placed a soothing hand onto his back. She nodded as he whispered something to her.

"We're gonna leave her here," Faith decided and looked closely at Bible. "Why are you called Bible?"

"I am Eustace Reed, ma'am," Bible replied. "I called Bible cuz know all the Bible."

He stated it matter-of-factly, not as a boastful answer.

"You take care of my Rose?" Faith ordered more than requested.

"Bible takes care with his life," Bible stated, showing her a powerful fist banging up against his chest like King Kong. "When boss says to crush Rose Rice's enemies… Bible used the hammer of God so Rose Rice free from all tyranny."

Bible had tears of anger in his eyes.

Joker walked up to him and squeezed his huge shoulder. "Hey B, wanna go bring Rose Rice out here?"

"Sure boss," Bible nodded and exited.

"He's very intense," Faith observed.

"Oh yeah," Joker agreed. "I have nine children and I can't believe the power he was with them. He's a gentle giant but he'll smash heads if anyone threatens those he loves."

When Rose entered the living room with Bible at her side – he wore a T-shirt now – her parents were instantly overcome with emotion. Rose Rice hesitated at first but rushed into their arms seconds later.

Joker left them alone. He made his way to the kitchen to see what the estate chef was preparing for lunch. There was a professional staff of Jamaican cooks and caterers that maintained the kitchen and served the meals. He had a word with the cook and then sat down out in the grand dining room at the head of the 30-seat gleaming white granite-top table.

Leah appeared wearing a delightful sky-blue YSL sundress with a black and white flower print. "Daddy! Two real quick things. Don Braga's been calling you about the drone thing."

He called Don Braga in Chicago right away. "Hello!"

"You on an encrypted line?" Don Braga asked.

"Course."

"My people been watching our boy via drone per plan," Don Braga reported to him. "His wife as well, that Valoria, various cartel associates of theirs, and a couple of others. We have addresses now on everyone and trackers on their vehicles."

Joker was happy to hear it. "*Extremely* great news. Send all drone cam footage, addresses, and everything else you got to me."

"Already done," Don Braga said. "Hey, did you know these fuckers have been opening tattoo parlors in the same vicinities that youse have strip joints?"

Joker let that news sink in.

"Yeah," Don Braga said, hearing Joker's thoughts, his rage. "It is not a coincidence that Albanian tattoo shops open everywhere you have a club established."

"In Chicago?"

"No, my friend. All throughout your route."

The entire meth alley, Joker thought. "So that's been the plan of betrayal all along. They tried to murder me to cement it. Aight. There's only one answer for all of it."

"Take care of yourself," Braga urged him.

"I plan on it," Joker stated. "One more thing."

"Shoot."

"Can we weaponize those drones you have?"

"You mean with explosives?"

"Yep."

Don Braga chuckled. "Can money buy diamonds?"

"We'll talk soon, Don Braga."

They hung up.

Joker looked at Leah. "My bad baby, you had somethin' else to tell me?"

Leah nodded. "Tithi is out of her coma," she quipped.

The food servers bought out a delicious lunch of Jamaican beef patties, saltfish salad, fruit salad, and buttered potato bread. Everyone was called in to eat the mid-day feast: Nina, Nyomi, Brayson, the Donohue's, Ariel, Kalani, Joker, his nine wives and children, and Bible.

During lunch, Joker's mind was elsewhere so he hurried through his meal. He used a napkin to wipe his mouth, threw it onto his plate, and excused himself.

"What happened with him?" Uzenna asked Leah.

"A lot," Leah sighed. "Tithi is out of the coma."

Uzenna lost her appetite.

CHAPTER SIXTEEN

Don Braga Safehouse
Chicago, ILL
Midnight Thursday

Nina silently observed Joker and Bible as they assembled and then disassembled twin rifles before returning each component back into its own carrying case.

"Those are some serious toys y'all got there," Nina mentioned from where she sat perched on a barstool inside of a luxury condominium owned by Big Frank Braga which they were inhabiting for the time being.

The condo was located in an upscale section of the city's east end. Joker had returned to Chicago to hear Tithi's side of things about the attempted assassination. Nina would be on hand to listen as would Nyomi, Malek, and Brayson Bailey who led the FBI's investigation. Joker had only brought Bible and Uzenna along with him to Chicago.

"Yeah, real serious," Joker responded as he peered through the barrel of the silencer which came with the weapon. "This is the -"

"Bolt action M-RAD sniper rifle," she finished for him. "With the

.338 modified wildcat ammo that spins for a truer hit. It's an assassin's dream piece. It's beautiful."

Joker nodded and turned to Bible. "Put these with others, son."

"Boss?" Bible hesitated.

Joker looked at Bible carefully. "What is it?"

"Remember that pretty girl I like?" Bible inquired.

Joker looked puzzled. He didn't know what or who the hell Bible was talking about. "The one from The Chi wit the phat ass?" Joker guessed.

Bible shook his head. "Bible like one woman and he don't have no children. Bible God-fearin' man, a warrior of God, and will be faithful to the woman he bless me to -"

"Spit it out, Bible man," Joker urged. "We all tired."

Bible took a deep breath. "Bible want wife."

Joker was startled for a moment. "What? Okay…Okay, I'm buggin' right now. What am I missin', son?"

"He in love."

"Who's in love? You?" Joker queried.

Bible nodded.

"Wit who? How? When? Where?" Joker removed his combat boots as he sat down on the foot of the bed in the only bedroom in the residence.

"Yolie Santana," Bible stated, trying to pull up a photo of her on his encrypted cellphone.

"The Puerto Rican girl?" Joker asked. "The EIE dancer?"

"Yeah," Bible answered. "You know Yolie. My Yolie."

Joker had to do some thinking. Yolie was one of the EIE standout strippers. She was bad. Really, really, hands down- cold-blooded ass – bad which was what had Joker worried. Yolie was about the cash. There ain't nothing wrong with that but Bible was different than his other men. Whether it be Bonecrusher, Hard Knox, Divine, Meth Man, or any of them. Bible was the squad's greatest fighter, its most prolific weapon, but he – ironically – needed protecting now.

Well, at least his heart did. The last thing Joker wanted for Bible was a woman to come in and fuck his head up. Bible man had been doing really good. No psychotic breakdowns. He took a litany of medications prescribed by his psychiatrists for his various conditions: auditory hallucinations (he heard voices). Paranoia (he constantly felt like people were out to get him.) PTSD (he would experience the shakes and adrenalin levels of a man who'd just witnessed another man getting his head chopped off by an Al Qaeda executioner).

"Of course, I fuckin' know Yolie," Joker acknowledged as he took off his pants and socks. Uzenna was already half asleep, laid out underneath the covers, on the bed. Joker stretched out on his back next to her. "Aight… so youse in love with Yolie. How?"

"Bible am."

Joker had a lot to think about with this Tithi situation tomorrow and Bible was in here talking about how he was in love with a high-end hoe. Not only that, he wanted to marry her, too. But Joker had to deal with Bible and his fixations extremely carefully. One wrong move could send the nigga spiraling in a direction he didn't want him to go.

Joker's eyelids were getting heavy.

"Guess I'll take the floor," Nina murmured as she walked into the lavish bedroom with a stack of neatly folded blankets and pillows. "You can join me, Bible, if you wish."

Although it was nearly Summer, it was cold inside of the building and the only air that came from the ventilation system was cool air. And since this particular condominium unit only had one bedroom, with one bed, Nina had no problem with taking the floor.

Joker sat back up. "Nah. No need for all that. We came to the Chi incognito. This is Don Braga's Mafia fortress building. Mafia lieutenants, captains, and their wives all live in it. The doormen are all killaz. Don Braga gave us two condos. Bible go across to your own condo and get a good night's sleep."

"The marriage to the love of my life?" Bible inquired as if he were a 16-year-old in need of his father's permission before he did it.

"Nina, come on and get in, doll baby," he patted the bed. Then he looked hard at Bible. "Son, you don't need my permission to get married."

Bible paused in the doorway. "Bible man knows he need not his boss' permission, sir. Mo like Bible man seeketh his boss' approval."

Nina undressed and slipped under the covers next to a lightly snoring Uzenna.

"I support and approve of any woman you choose for a wife as long as it ain't none of mine." He said. "But Yolie Santana from EIE, right? The Yolie we've known, loved, and cared for the last coupla years?"

Bible showed Joker a few of the young beauty's Instagram photographs.

"She's beautiful," Joker commented. "Y'all been in contact, B?"

Bible nodded. "Yes, sir."

JOKER LOOKED AT SOME OF THE OTHER PHOTOS BIBLE HAD STORED OF Yolie and nodded. Joker thought a while back to that time when Uzenna had called up some recruitments she'd known on the stripper circuit. That had been subsequent to the epic success the EIE Army had had in taking out Big Frank Braga's six Mafia bosses.

There had been some partying and celebrations poppin' off as a result of that success and Joker remembered grabbing Yolie's attention that night like it was yesterday… It went down like this:

"Hey, baby," he whispered to her. *"Why don't you take my man Bible to the hotel with you? The nigga ain't had a woman in years."*

She looked over at him. "I can see why. He's a monster."

Joker nodded. "But no one in the world is more loving or loyal. You can't do wrong doin' me a favor."

"You owe me big, man." She told Joker before walking over to Bible.

"Y'all been seein' each other – in a relationship?" Joker questioned him.

"Bible been courting Miss Yolie," Bible told him.

"Not that it's my business but I didn't know," Joker stated. "Anyway…I approve, son. Grab the key to the condo straight across from here. It's on the counter son-son."

Bible took the key and exited.

Joker laid next to his wife and within seconds, her soft curvy body was in the spoon position with his own. He wrapped his strong arm around her like an octopus, smelling the sweet scents wafting up his nostrils from her hair and face…

CHAPTER SEVENTEEN

Don Frank Braga's Safehouse
Chicago, ILL
12:05 AM

Joker had had plenty of sleep on the flight in and he'd slept solidly the evening prior to leaving Florida. After what Bible had just said to him about wanting to be married there was no way he could sleep now.

With everything that was going on Joker could not have Bible marrying a chick who was not being sincere with him. He hoped to God that Yolie wasn't going to break his heart because the heart was connected to the head. In Bible's case, if his heart was destroyed, his head would tell him to do something that American society was not ready for.

Joker sat up against the pillows on the large Queen- sized bed, his thoughts racing. He looked around the room which was dimly lit by the bedside light. Whoever had decorated it for Big Frank had been very thoughtful. It was immaculate and sumptuous without being overly expensive.

Joker reached for his cell phone and looked up Yolie's number. He called her and she answered on the second ring.

"*Olá*," her sultry sexy feminine voice said.

"It's me," he said, getting up. "You busy?"

"No," she said tiredly. "You need somethin'?"

He gave her the address to the condo. "Don't call nothin'. Don't say nothin'. Just come now."

"*Tambien*. Fifteen minutes."

She was there in more like twenty but the Killaz at the door downstairs buzzed her on in once her black Mercedes was parked in the underground garage across the street. Joker let her in with a happy hug. He got right to it and pulled out a stack of crispy $100 bills.

"Imma keep it one thou witchu, mami," he said as he sat down on the sofa. He only wore a pair of black Balenciaga shorts with an open bathrobe. "I'm tryna get it in. I'm tryna fuck. Straight up."

Yolie was looking edible, delicious, succulent, juicy, phat, tasty, and all that fly shit written about in all the Lou Garden Price Sr, "HITTAZ" and "SOSAFROMSCARFACE" novels on Amazon. She had thick, really full, and bouncy shoulder-length hair that was naturally black but had blond streaks in it. She was only 5 feet 5 inches tall but she was 158 pounds with the softest most unbelievable curves ever.

When Uzenna was working at the Villa she was the club's superstar stripper. That's because Uzenna was just that bad. Even to this day, of all the women inside or associated with the EIE organization, nothing had changed. Uzenna was without a doubt the baddest bitch. But, when it came to all the females who were still stripping for EIE and part of helping that cash come in from the meth profits, Yolie was #1 now.

Joker was aware of Yolie's 'boss' status. That was no secret. However, he had no idea that Yolie and Bible were still seeing each other. So he had to 'test' it and check it out for himself.

"Whatchu mean, Papi?" She said as he encircled her waist when she sat next to him.

He went in to kiss her lips and she moved away.

"I mean, you know my spending power, mama," Joker offered. "Gimme a number and let's do it."

"Me and you never did dat, Papi," she pushed him back a little. "I thought you called me over to make a money move."

"I did, sweet thang."

"You tryna fuck," she said with a smile. "I coulda brought my niece over," Yolie told him. "She nineteen and still a virgin but she dyin' to lose it… I can still call her. She will be all over you."

"Whatchu playin' hard to get?" Joker chuckled as he let her go. He didn't want to get too touchy or pushy. That would creep out any woman. "I tell you what…"

He baited her with that and let it hang.

He was her boss after all and she had two car notes and a mortgage now. The last thing she wanted to do was piss him off and have her cut from the team. Not when she was making $30,000 a month…

"Tell me what?" She asked finally.

"I said gimme a number," Joker stated as he picked up a pen off of the nearby glass coffee table. He wrote a five-figure number down on a napkin and gave it to her. "Can you use that each month whether we fuck or not?"

"Jesus," she laughed. "Hell yeah – if it's charity, J.R. But I just can't. I have a man now."

"He ain't gotta know," Joker told her.

Yolie was real sweet about it. "That ain't it. God will know. I'll know. You'll know."

"How long you been wit him?"

"A year," she revealed. "Faithful for nine months. You don't know who my man is?"

Joker sat forward and stood up. "C'mere, shorty."

She looked at him strangely. "What? *Que pasa, hombre*?"

He embraced her with a strong hug. He stroked her thick hair and kissed her cheeks a half dozen times. "I love you, ya heard, mami?"

"Yeah, I love you too Redman, but why you acting weird, Papi?" She asked.

He told her everything, point by point. Bit by bit.

"You fuckin' asshole." She laughed afterward. "Why you gon' try to play me like a roach bitch for? You wrong for that shit, Red."

"Why y'all bein' all secretive and shit?" Joker probed. "Bible's my peoples for real. My blood comrade."

"You know why," the sexy Boricua stated. "The first time we fucked was in New York when you asked me to and he only wanted to cuddle."

"At the Hyatt up there, right?" Joker was laughing but was interested as Nina and Uzenna came into the living room. He explained everything to catch them up.

"I think that was the Grand Hyatt," Uzenna added to the story. "Go 'head, Yoyo."

"We fuckin' cuddled but these bitches said he stretched me out, fucked me up – all sorts of dumb ass shit," Yolie informed them. "The bitches who ain't really know who I was, was sayin' that I had to be watched because if I'd fuck Bible man, I'd fuck any man. Just to be talkin' and teasin' until I put them Glocks down them hoes' throats."

"If you don't mind…" Joker paused. "When did y'all start fuckin'?"

Yolie shook her head. "We never did."

Joker was surprised. "Whaaat? Never? Y'all wanna be married?"

Yolie started laughing, "Oh. We've done everything except intercourse."

"I was about to say," Uzenna said, nudging the raven-haired Latina. "How would a girl know what her husband-to-be was workin' wit? We got a right to see it beforehand at best."

"How soon did you see it?" Nina had a desire to know.

"He was so sweet to me," Yolie started to tell the story. "That next night. But even though Red wanted me to give myself to him for an evening of fun… he didn't want sex. He brushed my hair and told me how perfect I was. Not 'pretty' or how big my 'boobs and ass were. Nothin' vain that all other guys use… he just spoke of perfection and how the Lord loves me. On the second night, he helped me with a pedicure. He painted my toenails, he massaged me, and sucked my toes until I orgasmed."

Nina's mouth was open. "That's when you saw it?"

"Seen what?" Yolie queried. Then… "Oh, that. You CIAs never get any?"

Nina frowned. "That's the truth. Ninety-seven percent of the agents I know that have marriages, they end in divorces."

"That's sad," Uzenna blurted.

"I'm a hairy Puerto Rican girl," she admitted with a shrug. "So I busted out the Bath and Body Works beauty kits and let him spread this new depilatory all over my entire body."

"Depilatory? What's that?" Nina wanted to understand. "You mean like a Nair?"

"That's it," Yolie said. "He spread it everywhere. Between my butt cheeks, my coochie, underarms, over my legs, arms, back – every inch of me. Lemme tell you. That man had me reciting Psalm 23 while he removed the hair from my body. He baptized me in my own bathtub. He took me out, my skin was tingling, and treated it with soothing cocoa butter. We were just two lovers kissing. Beautiful, hot, wet, kisses with many whimpers and moans… I pulled off all of his clothes… you want to hear this, Joker Red?" She looked past Uzenna at Joker.

Joker Red shrugged. "Go head, mama. That's my fuckin' dude so…"

"When I first saw how big and solid of a man he was, I was like 'he probably got a peewee dick'," Yolie laughed. "No offense, Uzenna, but we all lust behind ya husband's back about that porno horse dick he got. I was hopin' for fuckin' once – just once – I catch a break. I never get the man I want with at least seven inches. Maybe even six if it's nice and thick. A bitch is always gettin' surprised by men I like with baby dicks. Morenos- Black men, with long dicks but they be pencils. Too skinny."

Uzenna and Nina were cracking up because that was the truth. Men had it good. They could actually see the woman's body in most cases. The curves and contours and – in some instances – her pussy imprint. Men knew what they were getting.

"Bible is truly a man crafted by God," Yolie revealed. "He already had me singing praises… I held in my hands the biggest but hairiest dick I'd ever seen. So, what I did was use my magic shave depilatory cream on *his* body. I lathered and removed it all. Oh my God… it was a huge mountain of warm chocolate from there. He had the most beautiful dick. Without all that hair that encircled it like a Christmas wreath, it's sexy and oh-so-smooth. His scrotum is a tennis ball."

"You are very descriptive about that man's dick," Joker stated, making everyone laugh. "How long is it?"

Yolie smiled. She had a clean white smile with beautiful gum lines. "I literally asked him to let me measure it and it's eleven and a half inches."

Uzenna and Nina giggled.

"God," Uzenna said. "I know you was intimidated by that shit."

Yolie admitted that she was. "We dry humped and I gave him head like he never had before. I nearly choked as I sucked his enormous dick. It's so thick I couldn't even get it in my mouth. But I used a sweet-flavored edible lubricant to help. When I made him cum the first time, I did my best to swallow all of his cum but it might as well shoulda been a whole raw egg worth."

Uzenna was laying on the sofa with her head in Joker's lap and she could feel how hard he had come at hearing Yolie's detailed story. The large plum-sized dickhead poked out above Joker's waistline and Uzenna could not help but to kiss it when she saw it rise in his shorts. Hungry for her man, Uzenna pulled the waistline down and she captured the head of the beast in her mouth and slowly slavered her tongue in dozens of swirls and twirls that sent jolts of electricity to the pulsating nerve-endings inside of his billowing scrotum.

Yolie and Nina watched the live "XXX Action" show unfolding before their very eyes. Yolie's nipples were so hard that they hurt but "hurt so good." She sent Bible a text because she'd been told that was asleep across the hall.

"Let's go back to bed, Daddy," Uzenna whispered as Joker pulled her close to him and kissed her.

She dipped back down, taking his granite hard lumber in her left hand and eating the pre-cum that oozed out from the head.

"I can taste the honey in your balls, Daddy," she moaned, looking up as Bible entered. "Mm, hi, Bible, we got horny and couldn't sleep."

"I see." Bible hugged Yolie tightly.

Uzenna was pulling on Joker. "C'mon, Daddy…"

"Hey, Bible?" Joker said.

"Yeah, boss?"

"Yolie a good girl, homie," Joker told him. "Imma pay for y'all weddin'."

"I'm horny for you, my killer priest," Yolie whispered in his ear. "I want you to fuck my breasts and my face."

Bible picked her up like she was a ragdoll and carried her out of the condo.

Uzenna pulled her husband into the bedroom, leaving Nina out on the sofa with creamy panties…

CHAPTER EIGHTEEN

Don Braga's Safehouse
"Creamy Panties"

With both of them now stripped completely bare Uzenna laid his fine yellow ass back on the bed pillows and spread his legs wide. She positioned herself onto her stomach and softly clutched his huge shaft while sword swallowing it – or at least attempting to. She kissed the beast all along the veiny sides and nuzzled her nose and face down into his clean-shaven balls. She waited for another small stream of pre-ejaculate to eject in slow motion from the tip of his corona and she smeared it all over her lovely lips.

"Go get her," Uzenna whispered. "I saw it in her eyes: her pussy's in flames."

Joker nudged her. "You do it."

Uzenna got up and went out into the living room. The beautiful, chocolate-skinned CIA agent was laying out there on the red leather sofas with her panties pulled to the side, her right pointer and ring fingers thrusting deeply inside of her sopping wet sugar canal while her pink clitoris was being titillated, squeezed, and pinched by the first three fingers of her left hand.

"Uhhh, oh my God." Nina gasped out her pleasure when Uzenna appeared and grabbed her by the left forearm.

"C'mere, Hershey's kisses…" Uzenna said, pulling her up off of the sofa. Nina's white t-shirt dropped back down over her chocolate brown buttocks as she was led into the large bedroom by Uzenna.

Nina saw Joker Red's sexy, muscular, body laying there on the bed with all these amazing and expensive tattoos from his neck down to his legs. But, for the moment, what stood out the most and beckoned to her was his infamously large manhood. The thing he called the 'the beast' made a woman salivate. It had a curve in it and looked to be about a foot long. Red never bothered with a true measurement because what would it matter anyway?

"There you are," Joker said while looking at Nina. "C'mere, baby."

She was so horny now that nothing could stop her. She crawled up onto the bed and he removed the t-shirt she wore along with the panties.

"Her fingers was all in the pie," Uzenna told him as she came up behind the sexy CIA Agent. "Her pussy scent is all in the air out there."

"Yeah? Gimme those fingers," he said to Nina after pulling her lithe athletic body to his own and kissing her on the mouth.

Nina placed her hands to his nose and he moaned, "Mmmm," as he caught her pussy scent on her fingers.

He laid a hot kiss on Nina, sucking on her lips and tongue to take in her deliciously sweet taste. She tasted so good that he had to share her with Uzenna. All of Uzenna's female sensuality emerged when the two women kissed, Nina was instantly enamored with the younger Uzenna. Nina took both of Uzenna's hands and pinned them above her head with Nina's left hand. Nina spread open her own gash, exposing her extended clitoris, and thrust her tongue into Uzenna's mouth as they mashed and locked their pussies together.

Uzenna opened up wider and pulled Nina down harder by the lower back and buttocks as Uzenna grinded up into her in circular gyrations. Nina caught the left lower back and right ass cheek of Uzenna and the two women were locked tight into each other and wasn't going to let go. They were two hot, thrashing, fucking bodies. Nina's lovely ass could be seen better because she was on top. But they sort of leaned over to the right but each woman's wet pussy was kissing and grinding up wetly against the other's.

Somehow, Uzenna managed to pin Nina on her belly and Uzenna was humping her ass as if she had a penis but that wasn't it. Uzenna's clit was so extended that once it felt the firm right buttock of Nina, she was able to get off on it by fucking herself back and forth off it. Uzenna was able to set off fireworks in Nina that she never thought she had. Uzenna loved trapping Nina's clit in her mouth and making the dark brown agent come undone.

Joker was glad that Uzenna was able to cause Nina to "fall apart" with pleasure because when it came down to her taking his massive organ inside of her, she was unable to do it.

"Damn, Nina, that coochie is just too tight," he said after trying for the last time. "Don't worry, baby. It's happened before. No big deal."

So, before they fell asleep, Nina and Uzenna finished him off with their mouths. He spurted streams of warm cum all over their breasts before they fell asleep together in an exhausted heap.

PART TWO

There's some ugly shit goin' on in America. If killaz can roam in secret, then the only way to stop them is with a secret army of killaz.

CHAPTER NINETEEN

Chicago Memorial Hospital
10:30 AM

Tithi could not bring herself to look into his eyes. The interview was conducted inside the basement level of Chicago Memorial Hospital. Joker was dressed in a custom-made gray silk suit. He was offered a seat but he opted to stand up during the entire meeting.

Inside of the room, as previously discussed, was Nyomi Malek (FBI), Joker Red, Nina Overstreet, and Brayson Bailey. In the hospital corridors, outside of the room they were having the meeting in was a group of HRT which was the FBI's version of SWAT. They were the most elite squadron of all inside of law enforcement. The "Hostage Rescue Team" were a fearless squad of highly trained and well-organized assassins with badges. They were all dressed in U.S. Army camouflage with "FBI-HRT" bands around their bicep area and on their bulletproof vests.

"Start from the beginning, Tithi," Joker said, cutting right to it.

The right side of her face was covered with a thick layer of some kind of ointment. Likely a Vitamin A and D ointment or something mixed with cocoa butter. Her facial burn was profound and plainly visible. She was in serious pain. Joker approached her bedside and wanted to get a look at her injuries with his own eyes. She was still hooked up to the monitors, all the conventional equipment, so medical personnel could keep a good watch on her. For the most part, she had been coming along nicely.

Joker slowly and gently removed the bandages that were covering her torso. "They couldn't save your right breast, huh, Tithi?" He asked and answered all in the same breath.

She shook her head slightly. Her facial burns were so devastating that the left eyelid had been seared off and he inspected her other limbs and torso.

"What's your name?"

"Tithi," she said to him, her voice weak, sad.

He nodded. "Time is money. TALK. We know you can talk. You just said your name. Who approached you?"

"A Latino," Tithi admitted. "No name. He caught me coming from work. In the parking lot at Rocio's, I always stop at Rocio's for tea after work."

Joker looked at Brayson who sat with his laptop open. "Rocio Mastriana. She's a restaurant owner, southside Chicago for thirty years. No record."

Joker made a phone call. "Hello, hello…"

Apolina answered. "I'm glad you called."

"Really?" Joker said. "Glad you answered."

"Check what I sent you," the young Apolina Noriega directed him. "Then I'm done, man! I'm fuckin' done!"

He sensed alarm or something in her voice. "Okay. Where are you? Why you buggin' out?"

"They're gonna kill me!" She told him.

He didn't have time for this. "What happened? Who?"

"Honey B knows, J.R., she *knows*," Apolina informed him.

"That you been spying?" Joker said quickly.

"Yeah, what else? Shit. Move." She screamed at someone in the background. She must be driving. "Yeah Joker, Honey B fuckin' knows."

"How? How da fuck do she know anything?" Joker snapped back. "What'd you fuckin' do?"

"I fucked up, man… God, I fucked up!" Apolina cried. "I was puttin' it all together and I knew you was waitin'…"

"And?"

"I accidentally texted it to her phone."

Joker's stomach flopped and flipped and felt like he had to fart or take a shit.

"Ge out now." He told her. "Call 9-1-1 or something cuz I can't help you, you dumb bitch."

"I'm out but I have they fuckin' files." She said frantically. "I stole all of them. I think I know where Honey B been hidin' her kid she had wit El Verdugo."

Suddenly, the call went dead. It dropped or something. Joker looked at Nina, Brayson, and Nyomi. "Hallway… *Now!*"

The four of them rushed out into the corridor- out of earshot of the HRT – where Joker attempted to decipher Apolina's phone call.

"She has an encrypted device?" Brayson inquired.

"Yeah," Joker responded. "She's on our network so we can follow her."

Brayson nodded. "Is there somethin' else?"

Joker's mind was racing. "Maybe Apolina discovered the mother of all bombs when it comes to secrets in this relationship. She found out where Honey B's been hiding her child with cartel assassin El Verdugo."

Brayson stood stock still. "Hiding?" He repeated. "Why would a woman hide a child from a previous relationship from her current lover?"

"Her current *husband*," Nina informed him. "They're married and she is now pregnant with Steven 'Ghostman' Adams' child."

Joker was talking in a low voice but he was clear. "Apolina, according to what she has been able to deduce, heard from Honey B herself that her leverage over Ghostman was that she has him on video committing the most shockin' murders one can see recorded..."

Right there in the corridor, Joker accessed one of the video messages that Apolina had been able to get her hands on. The two FBI agents, the CIA agent, and Joker watched the video of Ghostman having sex with Esmeralda Cartegena and then killing her.

Brayson was stunned.

"This vile woman enjoyed it," Nyomi said, astounded. "She had sex with him after."

"Jesus Christ." Nina shook her head.

Joker showed them another video. "This girl was reported missing."

"Okay, I remember Daphne Jessoms," Nyomi said as they watched the sex video. "Beautiful, beautiful, teen girl. The freckles and the eyes. Is this a homicide?"

They watched and saw the pill that the teen was duped into taking by Ghostman. He had told her that it was ecstasy and feigned as if he was going to take one with her but he didn't. Daphne Jessoms never woke up and was never found alive or dead.

"Steven Adams..." Brayson said with disdain in his voice. He looked at Joker. "You know him best. Is he a serial killer?"

Joker looked right back at him. "Do we count the ones the U.S. government ordered him to kill or the two we just saw here on video?"

Brayson didn't push it any further. "Okay... the child she had with El Verdugo. How's this and the murders all tie in?"

"It's how Honey B took control," Joker Red stated knowingly. "She used the videos to blackmail Ghostman. Let's pick up Apolina and once we have her, we'll have the entire story."

"The child," Nina said as she dialed a number. "Let's get that child in the meantime because if she went through all of that to literally hide her kid then she truly believed that the man she married would murder the child..."

"Lord have mercy," Nyomi muttered as the thought really sank in. As Nina spoke on the phone, Nyomi said to Brayson, "Have you really processed how twisted this case has become? A woman, a mother of a…"

"*Son,*" Joker filled in the blanks loud enough so Nina could hear also because she was on the telephone with Lieutenant Sampson Gates. "Initially, the son – who is between seven and nine years old now – traveled to Santo Domingo with a relative or nanny but financial records suggest Brazil…"

"How on earth does a mother see fit to protect her son from being murdered on the one hand…" Nyomi was elaborating. "She gets him safe- far, far away in the Dominican Republic. Presumably with thousands of bucks because her mom has big cartel cash, EIE cash. But only a few years later – maybe two years – she's about to have a baby by the lunatic mercenary who wants your son fuckin' dead."

"I don't have the capability to wrap my head around that level of senselessness," Brayson replied.

Joker returned to Tithi's room to finish up. "Aight. The Latino man said what?" Joker questioned her.

"They had my mom, dad, and brother hostage," she explained. "I was shown the torture video."

Joker nodded. "I seen it. The aconite plant. Whose idea?"

"Theirs," Tithi said, sounding credible. "We are speaking about the poppy and I said there were many bad plants. In my country, aconite flowers were beautiful but lethal. Honey B has an Albanian tattoo designer who designed my tiger cubs and aconite plant for three hundred dollars. It was only supposed to represent how close to extinction the Bengal tiger is in India. The aconite represents beauty and death. I could've just put a rifle and bullets but… the plant was prettier for a chick's tattoo. I never master-minded anything. But when I had the food, I know it was poisoned."

"The car outside of the war room," he questioned her. "Who was it?"

"Albanian hittaz," she said. "Demetri and Culli- somethin'."

"The Dodge Charger," he pressed. "On the highway. They shot me. Who were they?"

She shrugged. "I'm so, so sorry. I don't know."

"Yeah, you sorry aiight," Joker told her.

He questioned her for at least an hour with everything she said being recorded on video. They wanted to be able to gather as much information as they could because they wanted to cut the heads off of the Albanians. This was not a problem similar to the Italian/Sicilian problem of La Cosa Nostra from the Roaring Twenties through the 1990s. These Albanians… they had no rules. Joker's plan had always been to handle street shit on a street level. EIE was made up of executioners, not prosecutors. He wanted to find what he needed to find out and deal with it his way. So, he grabbed the digital camera off of the stand and sent all of the footage to his encrypted phone. Then he deleted the footage on the camera.

Turing the camera completely off, he turned to Tithi, "What kept you from coming to me?"

"I was so scared," she said.

He shook his head. "It was fuckin' aconite, Tithi. You was gonna fuckin' sacrifice *my life*?"

She was crying. "In Hindu… it is a greater sin to lose three lives I could save than to lose one."

He laughed and shook his head. "Tithi, Tithi, Tithi…"

Joker removed a .25 Derringer from his back pocket and placed it within her grasp. "Only one thing left for you to do huh? What more is left for you here? *Look at you.*"

She broke down in tears even more as she nodded her agreement with him. Nina quietly re-entered the room and observed the exchange. Tithi's left hand was bandaged but she tried to reach out for his left hand. It was kind of awkward so she tucked the Derringer underneath her pillow and used her right hand along with her left hand to hold his left hand in place.

"May I please have your word on my family's safety back to India?" She requested.

"They'll be on a plane very soon," Joker assured her.

"I'm so sorry, Joker," she whined.

She pulled his hand to her stomach and said nothing more. He pulled his hand away and walked out of the room. Nina stared at her for a moment prior to following behind Joker Red.

In the parking lot, Nina sat next to him inside of the sleek silver Suburban. "When she grabbed your arm like that... is she still pregnant, Joker?"

"I don't think she ever was," he replied stoically.

"I don't know, man," Nina stated in a way that made him think twice. "Better to make sure before you give her the suicide weapon and all... especially in her pain, high stress, depression, and whatnot. She'll use it."

Joker sat still for a second and then jumped back out of the Chevy Suburban. He walked back into the hospital and by the time they were on the basement level – where Tithi was at – there was pandemonium.

Tithi had already used the pistol to end her own young life. Joker didn't have to ask what had happened. That was as clear as day.

CHAPTER TWENTY

Flight to Brazil
Meth Man Ace

Meth Man Ace's hands wandered down the brown-skinned beauty's slender back as his thick lips brushed up against her throat. They were standing alone in the steward/stewardesses break area on the C-9 Skytrain II. Meth Man had met her when he'd first boarded the magnificent airplane at Juan Santamaria International Airport in Costa Rica.

He had been instructed at La Bella Marín Hotel. Meth Man and his wives had been busy the last several weeks moving the massive methamphetamine production operation to the Florida backwoods from their Illinois farms. Meth Man had already sent his four wives ahead of him to Campinas because he planned on staying in the country for a few weeks to relax, sightsee, and a lot more.

Blanca, Bambina, Natalya, Alejandra, and Ace were not exactly like Joker and his wives. They often went where the wind (the mood) took them. That meant Alejandra might bring a cute Japanese college student over and all five of them would have a go at her all weekend.

Or Meth Man would watch through a two-way mirror while a

really hot, tattooed, butch Latina would service one or more of his wives for days at a 5-star Chicago hotel. One thing they never did was bring these "extras" home. The sexy Puerto Rican tattooed butch girl was actually a stripper with a huge Instagram following of 100,800 people. Men and women were fascinated by her banging ass body and acrobatic moves.

"You know what I'd like to see?" Meth Man told his wives a couple of weeks back. "As much as y'all like to see me slay this big meat up in bitches…it'll only be fair if y'all fuck, too."

"Eww. You mean me and another man?" Bambina had recoiled. "We just had a son not that long ago."

Natalya, Blanca, and Alejandra also rejected the idea. At least when he'd first introduced it.

Meth Man Ace had known that they were just showing some modesty. "Bambi…havin' our son turned that hundred pounds of slammin' curviness to a hundred thirty-five pounds of insanity – head to toe. You turned into a porno queen in bed because your confidence grew. Say, I'm lyin'."

Bambina had giggled shyly.

"All y'all stop frontin'," he'd smooth-talked them. "The excitement of brand-new sex? A brand new juicy big dick to suck and huge balls to rub your faces in? I mean I love all y'all but each time y'all let me fuck and suck a new bitch, all that brand new excitement makes me full of somethin' that makes me crazy but I also feel more than lust. I feel selfish and guilty."

That had made his wives listen.

"Y'all like females but I know you like men even more," he'd told them. "So, we about to put the apartment wit the two-way mirror to more use…or let's hit a five-star hotel and set up a bachelorette party."

The women had laughed and delighted in that suggestion. They envisioned the hottest Black, Latino, and white male strippers…

"You get jealous when I'm slayin' nine inches of this thick ass meat balls deep in a badass strange bitch?" He had asked the brown-skinned Afro-Latina named Blanca. She had a small waist, a full phat ass, a cute round face, and stood at 5 feet 6 inches tall. Blanca was almost 30 years old and everywhere she went eyes followed her high-powered walk.

"I'm Dominicana," she'd said. "Of course, but you're like a porno movie. That's why I can watch and not touch."

"So how do you think I'd feel?" He'd told her while holding her tight and kissing her left ear. "Every man I see when you walk by be wantin' this little pussy you got. You like porn so I know you have dreams of fuckin' and suckin' someone new. You and Natalya be all on them lawn boys when they got they shirts off."

Natalya had giggled. "I like arms and butts so that's what I was lookin' at."

"Caught. Busted," Blanca had admitted. "Nothin' wrong with fantasizing."

"And y'all have my permission to do a little more," he had finally said to them. "If you want the privacy of it I understand that. But if you can get past the shyness then let us watch you without him knowin'. Cuz I'm not into dudes. Just live porn outta the women I've married. I won't be mad. We doin' it anyway wit women right?"

At the present, Meth Man Ace had been all over this lovely flight attendant from Brazil for the entire flight from Costa Rica. There was an instant attraction. Her name was Yajaira Carmona Soto; she was a light brown – like a leaf in the fall – and her eyes a few shades darker, sort of like Bustelo brand coffee with a little cream in it. She was 5 feet 7 inches tall, small waist, and an ass that made "Brazilian Butt Lift" so famous. As a flight attendant for Azul Brazilian Airlines, she had a choice to wear the company's blue dress, white blouse, and red tie uniform or she could wear the white blouse and red tie with the blue polyester slacks. For thin women, the slacks looked boyish but for females with hips and ass, the slacks were perfect. The male passengers salivated each time she walked by and some of them got in trouble with their wives.

"You are so bad," Yajaira whispered as the tall, light skinned man with the Brooklyn accent said something X-rated in her ear.

"Cuz youse a bad ass South American babe," he said as the 'SEAT BELTS ON' sign came on. "You know *La Bella* Hotel in Campinas?"

She sat next to him. "La Bella Marín, yes. That's the best hotel in the city."

He pulled out a thick stack of $100 bills and gave her $500. "That's for your cab and whatever else."

She didn't accept the money. "I'd be low-class to accept that. Plus, I have a husband."

"You ever cheat on him?"

She laughed. "I've come very close. Well… I sucked my boss's dick once. Why?"

"Well if you're gonna do it, why not do it with a man with four wives and an open relationship? My wives are very beautiful and will love you. We have the presidential suite at La Bella Marín for a week. We're very rich and love to party."

He showed her photos of his wives on his laptop.

"They're all Latina?"

He nodded. "Blanca's Afro-Latina. Do you have a brother or friend who won't betray you to your husband?"

She nodded. "My brother."

She showed Ace a photo of her brother.

Ace smiled. "Everyone's healthy? No diseases?"

"No way!" She exclaimed. "You guys?"

"Definitely clean," he told her. "You're thinkin' about it."

She smiled so prettily, it was almost heartbreaking. "You are so devilish. But cute. Then you drop this bombshell of four delectable wives…open marriage… I'm married, my brother is married, but I hate his wife."

She laughed as the plane started landing.

"In our sexual lifestyle my wives are not in it for one another," he said. "They let me bring hot babes in because it's such a turn-on to see me kiss and pound so much meat in and out of a woman. I get off on bein' watched."

Yajaira listened intently. "It's that good huh?"

He took her left hand, the one that sparkled with the gold wedding band and diamond engagement ring and placed it on the growing bone in his jeans. He put a jacket on top to conceal them and unbuttoned his pants. Then he guided her hand down inside of his boxers.

"Look at me, Yaya – can I call you Yaya?"

She nodded. "God, oh my – I can't believe I'm -"

"Touchin' such a juicy dick?" He whispered close to her ear. "I saw you today – that hot body and phat ass – and knew I had to have you. Husband? Fuck your husband. If you let me, you wanna be fucked and sucked real good?"

She was stroking that big ass dick now.

"Your husband dick that big?" He asked.

She shook her head. "He's like five inches. He got a daycare dick. This is…"

"I want you to sit that pretty ass pussy on my face," he said, cutting her short. "I know it'll feel good, taste good, as my thick lips and tongue drive that asshole crazy, your clit all insane and loosen up the drops of that pretty juice that's trapped inside cuz your husband's dick too tiny to buss it open like I can. My mouth wants your mouth. I wanna suck your titties. I want you to suck all on my dick and balls. I'd love to shoot mad cum in that pretty mouth. It'll stay hard. Real hard so I can bury it in that little pink hole you got. With an ass like yours, you runnin' around wit no dick in it. I'd love to butt fuck you."

"I wish I could suck that pre-cum flow you have," she whispered back, her thumb slowly brushing circles around the corona. "It's so big like I'm holding a twenty-ounce bottle of Pepsi or somethin'."

The plane landed and taxied to a halt.

"*La Bella Marín*, Mamita," he said as he buttoned up his clothes and kissed her for a full minute.

She pushed his hands away so he could let her go. "It'll be there." She felt her clit pulsing wildly.

They departed from each other.

Meth Man Ace walked out through the main entrance of Viracopos – Campinas International Airport and looked around. The parking lot was a zoo. At 2:00 PM there were taxis, van services, buses, cars, police vehicles, and more everywhere. He noticed a brand-new white

Mercedes waiting and then the front passenger side window came down.

"Get in here, boy," Natalya said loud enough for him to hear. She had a smile on her face.

Ace smiled, placed his suitcases into the trunk, and got into the backseat with Blanca and Bambina while Alejandra drove.

"Drive straight to the address we were given," he directed her.

"It's not far from here," Alejandra told him. "We actually looked at it driving by when we arrived yesterday. Well, let's take a look at it. We could get lucky and get this show on the road."

CHAPTER TWENTY-ONE

Joker and Nina
"Kidnapping Honey B's Son"

Joker was about to ignore the vibrating cell phone buzzing in his pocket but he didn't. He looked at the screen to see who it was…

"Ace," Joker answered as he sat inside of the rear passenger seat of one of the bulletproof/bombproof Denali's he had left inside of a storage garage in Chicago. "Talk to me, homie," Joker told him as the SUV was currently going through a full car wash.

"How soon can you have one of our jets sent down here to escort the boy back?" Ace inquired.

"You got'em?" Joker asked, some surprise in his voice.

Meth Man Ace answered him. "Not yet but there's no security. Just a woman in her fifties. The mailboxes says Bernyce Mejia at their house. Old girl found the school he goes to about a half mile from the house. It's a private school. See if Leah can learn anymore about it."

"Name and address," Joker directed him.

He texted Joker: *COLEGIO INTERNACIONAL DE EMPRENDE-DORES C.I.E. S.R.I., Calle Suarez Arana 203, Campinas, Brazil.*

"Got it," Joker said seconds later, "stay on deck."

Joker put him on hold as the SUV was being dried off by a crew of Mexican workers. Joker forwarded the text from Meth Man to Leah.

Joker rolled his window down. "All y'all c'mere."

The crew of four workers came around to his window and he handed each man a bill. They were happy as hell.

Nina drove off while he put the window up.

"I sent Meth everything I found about that private school," Leah told Joker when she called in to Joker's line.

"I'm on the line, Lee," Ace said. "Okay… so the school security is zero here."

"It ain't America in Campinas," Leah stated. "Um, is that it? The school is clean, basic Montessori type."

Joker cut her off.

"The plane is bein' fueled right now," Joker informed him. "You want it at Viracopos- Campinas International Airport?"

"Si, mufuckin' señor." Meth said. "So, we stayin' out dis bitch at least a month."

"That's a long time to take ya eye off of business," Joker cautioned, meaning the crystal meth business.

"Maaan – we got backups for da backups." Meth boasted about his stockpiles. "Son, the fuckin' key to life is findin' rest and relaxation in between the stresses. Spend somma that cash on sunshine, bitches, and chillin'."

"You right, nigga," Joker acknowledged. "How's the wives?"

Meth had to sneeze. "Pardon self. All is well. We openin' up the marriage a little more. Me myself don't do dudes but I know bitches be wantin' new dick and balls to be nasty wit. So Imma let 'em fuck."

Joker actually surprised Meth with his reply. "Yeah, I'm no fool either. I'm married to a gang of bitches whose pussies turn into the ocean from a little bit of kissin'. They get horny as fuck when we watch porno flicks… or don't let me put the fuck scene on in *Monster's Ball* when Hallie Berry gets fucked by Bill Bob Thorton. But soon as you ask one of your babes if she wants new dick, they scrunch they faces all up."

"Bitch be lyin' like a mufucka!" Meth Man agreed. "Word ta fuckin' God, son."

Joker chuckled. "Son…it's eight to nine fuckin' billion people on the planet. The human was not made to be wit' just one single human. Specifically, man or men cuz inside of one nut, one male orgasm, exists about a quarter million live sperms. We was built to populate the earth and any new planets we end up findin' down the line. The female was only built to attract man, have him cum inside of her, and carry a limited amount of kids throughout her baby-birthing years. Once she's done she's done. A man can continue to buss nuts inside of other women and produce more children to the death."

Meth Man was 100% on board. "I know damn well that the buck didn't stop wit me on my wives seein' another nigga and bein' like *'ooouu, girl, I know damn well that cat would have me squirtin' juice all over his dick and balls.'*"

"They want sex more than guys," Joker stated wisely. "Wit your deal, y'all are mad different than us. My wives were street smart girls from real early ages."

"God bless the dead," Meth said. "But outta the thirteen before Tithi, you had three Black girls and nine white ones. Coral Nee's Chinese. You lucky, dog."

"Why?"

"If that count was nine black and three white, it woulda never worked," Meth opined. "Black chicks would never go for that like White women. Them Black girls woulda never even gotchu to the hundred-thousand-dollar mark because Black Folks hate each other too much. It's a genetic defect. They woulda crossed each other and their pride woulda stopped your prison plan right on the tracks. These Blacks out here want five hundred-dollar wigs, six-hundred-dollar red bottom shoes, fifteen-hundred-dollar cell phones, bullshit, expensive Gucci and Louis Vuitton and trash clothes, jewelry and drinks their favorite rapper niggas or rapper bitches releases. Nine Black hoes woulda betrayed you, destroyed whatchu was buildin', set you up to get killed for a ring or watch or some petty-minded dumb shit like that. Black hoes are savages."

Joker liked Meth Man's thinking. "I haveta agree."

"Glad you do," Meth told him. "You got lucky. *Lotto lucky*, nigga. Cuz Uzenna was the bitch to keep the rest in order but one thousand percent credit has to be shown to the snowbirds you got. I bet it all on facts, son. Romie did you filthy, dirty, grimy, nasty. Coulda got A-Son so scared to get caught, he coulda ended you. *Dangerous treacherous bitch*. Her own blood had to throw da dirt on her because they were uncertain about their own futures. That's just my views. You know what's last?"

Joker replied. "Uzenna takin' Baby Joker."

"Add it all up, son," Meth urged him. "Them white women catapulted you to the top of the game. You redefined terms like 'player', 'king', or 'kingpin', or 'the Joker Red Syndicate', or shit like that…"

"Fuck titles," Joker told him just as Nina pulled over near the Morris Street subway station downtown. "EIE is the name of the people and the company. That's it."

Meth Man suddenly changed his tone. "Okay… he cool."

Joker didn't know what was going on…

"I got eyes, on the boy, son…" Ace whispered and paused. "Hold up…"

He was using a pair of high-end binoculars watching the front entrance of the school. Several cars at a time was pulling up and parking along the front sidewalk. They were parents there to pick up their children. At approximately 3:00 PM, Ace spotted Honey B's son come dashin' out of the front entrance with a group of other excited children who were happy to get released for the day. He watched as the boy waved goodbye to his friends and headed to a waiting Lexus SUV.

"Aight, son, get them wings here," Ace told Joker. "The nanny – Bernyce Mejia – is the only one who comes to pick him up."

"It's comin'," Joker reassured him. "Find a different city to vacation in afterwards. Once word is out that he's gone, Honey B's gonna send goons to investigate."

"Headed."

They ended the call right there.

Nina had driven them to a Wendy's where she'd placed an order and then retrieved it at the drive-thru window. By the time Joker hung up the phone Nina was already eating a chicken sandwich and a salad and Joker joined her.

While eating in the car, parked backwards in the farthest corner of the restaurant's parking lot, Leah called him…

"The Clipper will land at twenty-hundred hours Brazil time," she relayed the information. "Ace is aware."

"What else?" Joker asked.

"Tithi's parents have been sent to India," she said. "They didn't know what happened but I've made arrangements to have her remains sent to them. Is that okay?"

Joker sighed. "She belongs with them. To be buried as Hindu which was her religion… *as false as that shit is*."

"You need to get to the Twin Towers," Leah told him. "Apolina will be bottled inside of the panic room in the Penthouse Two. Be careful with that girl, Daddy. She has a gun and she's wacked out on something."

"How you know she's high?" Joker asked as he looked at Nina. "Twin Towers," he said to her.

Nina started driving.

"She-Daddy, I just know what bitches sound like when they all pilled up or methed up." She reasoned. "I know what I heard."

"Hm. Aight, baby. Thank you." He bit into a juicy burger and pointed. "Apolina's over there scared as hell."

"I'm wondering what more does she got?" Nina said aloud.

She drove towards the Twin Towers. "I don't know but that young girl's runnin' for her life."

CHAPTER TWENTY-TWO

The Twin Towers
Chicago, ILL

"Apolina is a true blood great granddaughter of General Manuel Noriega," Joker said as Nina drove towards the Twin Towers. "I knew she had steel in her blood when I first recruited her to be a spy. Hey, pull over at the D.Q. and let me see if I can get Bible away from Yolie from a minute."

Nina pulled the luxurious Denali up into the Dairy Queen parking lot and parked on the Lawrence Avenue side. He called Bible and ordered him to meet him at the Dairy Queen.

"Apolina in danger?" Bible repeated what he was told. "Bible movin', boss."

"Don't get followed," Joker warned him.

They disconnected.

"You have an entire army you can call to extract this girl," Nina said. "Why just us?"

Joker put his seat back and finished off a large Pepsi from Wendy's. "I told you we in the Chi incognito. Once I call my mob up here, I'm thinning out the security at all the strip clubs we have open all

143

throughout meth alley. Not just that, these streets talk. They see EIE movin' about, Ghost will know in five minutes. I want him to think we're duckin' out. All warfare is based on deception. The more I can make my enemies believe something that ain't true, the stronger I become in battle. Right now, them mufuckaz is tryin' to stay low just like me. So… we good, chocolate kiss."

She smiled at that.

He put his New York Yankee baseball cap down over his forehead to relax while they waited for Bible.

"He's here, J.R.," Nina said, nudging him with an elbow.

Bible was not alone. Uzenna drove the black Hyundai and Yolie sat up front with her. Uzenna backed the car up next to where the Denali was parked. Joker got out of the SUV and looked at the Hyundai.

"This car is like a soda can when it comes to .223, 7.62s and .45 caliber rounds, Uzenna," Joker said, criticizing the Hyundai they were in. "Uzenna and Yolie, I want y'all to park up on Logan and Sixty-Fifth and when I call, come in hot."

"Logan and … sixty-fifth. There's a police station on the corner there," Yolie said.

Joker pulled out the bulletproof vests and helped fit one onto Bible. They both strapped M-5 submachine guns onto their shoulders and double Glock holsters on their sides.

Joker looked at Uzenna and Yolie. "Matter fact, leave this death trap sitting here and y'all get in here. At least I know you'll be safe."

"But they don't even know we're here," Uzenna complained.

"I'm sure Bible told y'all Apolina's locked in one of the panic rooms at the Twin Towers," Joker mentioned.

"Yeah, so?"

"*So*? So, don't be naïve. Get in the truck." Joker snapped. "This chick stole extremely serious info on them and they suspect her… they know she took shit."

Once they were all geared up Joker and Bible got into the SUV and Nina drove the short distance to the Twin Towers.

Nina pulled into the parking lot and Bible and Joker jumped out of the SUV.

"Leave it runnin'," Joker said. "Doors locked, windows up, and, if Ghostman or associates show up, remember you're in a Level 6 vehicle. Bullet and bombproof." They slammed the passenger doors shut and beelined straight up to the penthouse where Apolina was holed up.

"I have a bad feelin' about this, boss," Bible stated as he looked around the parking lot. He only had a few moments to scan the two buildings. "Are girls still living in the second tower?"

"Yeah, it's all occupied," Joker told him as he entered the first tower, M-5 held out in firing position eye out ahead of the sights, ready for combat.

They weren't aware of it yet but Apolina had been spotted entering the building by someone who worked as an EIE dancer for Ethnicity Dance Company which was once managed by Honey B. In fact, that was where she had met the Panamanian beauty Apolina at. The EDC had recruited hundreds of girls for work inside of the EIE underground stirp club operation all throughout Meth Alley and paid handsomely to assist in distributing their high potent crystal meth not only inside of the cities and towns the clubs were in but also to the wider, international, clientele via the Dark Net.

Honey B had been able to convince a brown skinned babe named Sapphire to "double deal." Sapphire was a stripper that EIE had poached from Surreal Nightlife Chicago Strip Club. She was given the keys to a lovely penthouse apartment in the Twin Tower's – building #2. Although Sapphire mainly worked at one of EIE's legitimate clubs in Gary, Indiana now she still called the Twin Towers home which was where her mother and her two-year-old son stayed. Honey B and Ghostman had paid her $5000 just to install a high-definition security camera in her apartment's living room which overlooked the entire parking lot and entrance to building #1.

Check the camera footage, Sapphire had texted Honey B. *Isn't that Apolina entering building #1?*

Honey B had showed the text to Ghostman and Ghostman had sent six goons over there to snatch her up. However, when they'd arrive at the nearly vacant building, they had realized that it was not plausible to crash in every door to search for Apolina. So what they had chosen to do was cover the stairwells, the floors, and monitor any elevator movement.

Once they were inside the lobby of the building and standing next to the elevators, Joker paused.

"I don't like it either, B," Joker told him as called Apolina.

"Yeah, y'all here yet?" She asked quickly.

"We here, you aiight?" Joker inquired.

"Yeah, just come on."

Joker could hear the fear in her voice. "We comin' up. Could …"

Suddenly the light on the elevator started to blink. First, it hit on the sixth floor and as it passed each additional floor it hit on the fifth, then the fourth, then the third… it stopped on the second floor.

"We comin', baby, hold up." Joker pocketed his phone and looked at Bible. "Ayo, B… ain't nobody livin' on the second floor."

Bible's face turned into a snarl. "Yeah, boss, I think the enemy is here… *So, let all thine enemies perish, O Lord: but let them that love him be as the sun when he goes forth in his might.* Judges Chapter Five Verse Thirty-One. C'mon, son."

"Let's roll,"

As soon as Joker pulled open the door to the stairwell that's when the bullets started flying.

CHAPTER TWENTY-THREE

Battle at Twin Towers
Chicago, ILL

"Up, right!" Bible crouched down as he shouted.

Bible had taken a round center mass which would have knocked the air out of a smaller man but Bible was a bull. He immediately ran forward to get out of Joker Red's way.

Joker started bussing his gun up to the right where a Black man with braids, dressed in dark jeans and a black New York Yankees hoody, was firing on them with a gray Tech-9 that had a suppressor attached. From where he stood behind the railing on the second-floor level, he kept shooting at the fearless hulk-like beast advancing up the stairs. Bible had his M-5 close quarters combat weapon returning well-aimed bursts of automatic fire at him!

"Who da fuck is you mufuckaz?" The man who looked to be only about nineteen screamed as the hot bullets from Bible's weapon cut into his legs and abdomen.

Bible rushed him and slapped him down with the steel M-5. "*The Hallelujah Man, Eustace Reed*!" Bible knelt on his chest, almost crushing him. "How many of y'all is in the building, son?"

Joker stood watch. "He got a radio."

Bible looked at the young man. "Get on that radio and -"

"How many first?" Joker questioned.

"Six," the youth admitted. "Please, man, Ghostman hardly gives us any jobs. Don't kill me, man. I have a daughter."

"Get on that radio and tell them to come to stairway one, second floor, I got 'em. Just like that. You'll live," Bible promised. *"Only if you believe in Christ Jesus. Do you?"*

The boy nodded. "I do."

Bible nodded and sat him up against the wall. Joker searched him and found nothing but extra magazines for the Tech-9. Joker pocketed them and stuck the Tech-9 in his vest with a fresh clip in it.

"Make da call den, boy," Bible commanded him.

When Bible was in full war mode he was a monster and he believed at all times that the Lord God was with him, both he and God were cutting down heathen enemies together. In his mind he was invincible and shockingly, he seemed to be just that. When the young man had fired at him and even hit him once in the chest, it barely moved him and he'd came running at him and shooting at that boy like a bull with guns in its horns.

Trell-One looked at Bible's monstrous features. *"Come to stairway one, second floor... I got 'em, over."*

There was a quick response.

"Got who? Over," Blood-three queried.

"Two men came in wearing tack gear and I ambushed both, over," the boy explained.

"One of them I think is Joker Red," Joker whispered for him to say.

He immediately said it.

"Responding to stairway one, second floor, over," Blood-three gave the order.

"Now, you promised to let me live, the man reminded Bible."

"I did. But I meant with the Lord Jesus Christ," Bible said and used his brick like fists to pummel the man to death. Bible turned into a complete maniac as he delivered at least fifteen blows to Trell-One's face, causing his brain to bleed from his skull cracking in like watermelon.

Bible stood up and made the sign of the cross over his chest. "Amen."

Joker opened up the second-floor door and tapped Bible on the shoulder. "C'mon."

Directly across from the "EXIT" that led to the stairway was a laundry room. They hid inside of there with the lights off waiting to see if the other hittaz took the bait.

Within two minutes they heard a noise down the hallway to the right and a door close. Joker knew that the door which had shut was the door to stairway two. Joker heard the voices of several men walking briskly towards Joker and Bible's positions.

Joker pulled out two grenades and held them tight as Bible pulled the pins out for him and opened the door. Joker tossed them both out after a two-count release to shorten the time the men had to run. Bible slammed the door shit and ducked down next to Joker.

Two devastating explosions made the entire building shake.

KAAABBBOOOOMMMM!

KAAABBBOOOOMMMM!

"Let's go." Joker shouted.

Out in the hallway three young Black men were laid out like rugs dead and bloodied on the floor. One more was moaning and whimpering in excruciating pain from the agony the shrapnel was causing as it embedded itself in a hundred tiny pieces in his back and legs.

Joker walked past, dumping two close head shots into the back of his dome, ending his misery in an instant. "This way." Joker said, advancing forward.

As they approached the other staircase one more man, an older white man came out slowly with his gun pointed out of the door frame. Joker and Bible had their backs to the left side of the hallway where the staircase doorway was so the Albanian hitta couldn't hear or see them. Sticking that pistol first was what gave him away.

Joker reached out and grabbed the man's entire wrist just as his head was peeking around the corner. Joker had his hand in a death grip.

He yanked the gun out of his hand and the Albanian had no choice but to fight. But that's exactly what Joker lusted for. He loved hitting people and being hit. However, with Bible nearby, Joker's bloodlust would have to be put on hold. Bible reached around Joker and blasted a large gaping hole into the Albanian's left eye socket. It looked like a big yawning mouth with mad blood leaking out of it.

"I wanted his ass alive," Joker shouted.

"Bible follow order to kill enemies… he enemy?"

"Yeah, but-"

Bible cut him off. "Then Bible do righteous kill. Apolina, boss."

They ran up the stairs to the top floor and Joker used a combination key code to let him into the luxurious penthouse. "Watch the hall, son," Joker told Bible.

Bible stayed put as Joker walked straight to the back of the Penthouse. He stopped in front of the steel door where the panic room was flashing a small flashlight at the camera above the door.

"Apolina, c'mon out." Joker yelled. He couldn't remember the code to open this particular panic room. He was calling Leah up for her help when the door clicked. And Apolina came out armed with a vicious looking M-16. "It's me, Apolina, lower that fuckin' thing."

"You're gonna kill me!" She cried. "I know it!"

"What the fuck?" Joker's face had a serious frown on it. "Fuck you talkin' bout? C'mon, bitch. All the mufuckaz we just kilt to come rescue your ass?"

Joker stepped past her into the panic room and saw the crushed pills on the glass desktop. Leah had been dead on when she'd warned Joker that Apolina was on drugs. He wiped the rest of the pill dust onto the floor. When he came back out he threw Apolina her purse.

"Gimme that." Joker snapped, snatching the machine gun from her. "Where'd you even get a rifle like this?"

They were walking out of the penthouse and then down the stairs.

"I stole it from the house," she admitted.

They were nearly flying down the staircase now, floor by floor. It was time to go.

When they were nearing the lobby they heard shots being fired and Joker's heart sank. "Keep down." Joker ordered.

He looked at Apolina. "You know how to use that shit?"

Apolina pulled the clip out and slapped it back it in. Then she pulled the slide back on the right side and popped the lever, so it was off safety, "I'm the great granddaughter of a historic Panamanian General remember?"

Joker nodded and followed Bible to the front lobby windows. To the right of the entrance was a black Dodge utility van where two Albanian men were using to fire at Nina. Uzenna had gotten out of the Denali to help Nina. Both women were armed with handguns and were taking cover behind the Denali.

"I told them to stay in the fuckin' truck!" Joker growled. "That M-16 got an RPG on it?"

Apolina nodded.

"Trade me," Joker said.

Apolina switched guns with him and he checked the M-16 for the M-203 grenade inside of it. He opened up the door and let Bible run out to provide more cover fire so that they could get to the Denali alive.

Bible was out there letting off shots like it was the Fourth of July – the white America's Independence Day. Joker came out like the commando he was trained to be and took direct aim at the black van. He let loose with the M-203 grenade.

BBAABBBOOOOOOMMMMM!!!

The explosion was surreal to the residents who were watching it. The blast was a large fireball that ripped the van in two.

"Get her to the truck." Joker yelled.

Bible led Apolina to the safety of the Denali. Uzenna ran back inside as did Nina. Joker walked out into the middle of the parking lot and suddenly, a shot hit him in the lower quad in his leg. He took a deep breath and stared at the wounded Albanian man.

"You bastard." The dark haired, bleeding hitta cursed Joker as he laid on the ground still pointing a black 9mm Ruger at Joker. He was trying to fire the weapon again but it had jammed.

Joker walked up to him and kicked the gun away from him. "How many Albanians are there and why the fuck y'all after me?"

"Hundreds of us," the man said.

Joker stepped on his stomach which had been torn open by shrapnel that had blasted into him from the M-203 blast. Joker applied pressure to his wound. "Talk and I'll end your misery. Whose sendin' you? Who are y'all?"

"We are NJË…also known as ONE," he told Joker after he stopped screaming. "We followed Valoria here…"

Blood bubbled out of his mouth and he choked on it. Joker just shook his head and put a bullet in his face. Then he turned around and limped to the truck.

Nina peeled off once Joker was inside of the big SUV.

"Go! Go! To the safehouse." Joker ordered as he used a belt as a tourniquet to stop the bleeding in his leg. He used a stack of napkins to apply additional pressure. "Why the hell y'all leave the fuckin' truck?" Joker boomed.

"They were waiting to ambush the front when y'all came out," Nina explained. "We seen them come into the parking lot as clear as day. They must have been nearby. Because once those explosions went off…"

"That's when they came," Uzenna finished for her.

Joker and Bible still sat with their black demon masks on.

"Stop here, Nina," Joker told her. "Park between these two cars."

She did as he asked.

Once parked he stashed the firearms back into the custom-made stash behind the dash. They took off their masks and bulletproof vests and slipped on clean white t-shirts. They were both drenched with sweat. Bible switched the license plates.

"Y'all gotta come on," Nina hurried them.

They jumped back in the car. Nina looked behind her at Joker Red. "You're wounded bad?" She asked.

"Flesh wound," he said. "Nine-millimeter. It didn't strike the femoral artery."

Nina nodded. "Keep pressure on it."
They made it to the safehouse intact.

CHAPTER TWENTY-FOUR

The Braga Safehouse
10:45 PM
Chicago, ILL

Nina wasted no time sedating Joker Red and, with Bible's assistance, they were able to surgically remove the projectile from his thigh muscle. Bible stitched him up as Uzenna and Apolina looked on.

The last thing they did was manually bathe him, rinse off the soap, dry him, dress him in underwear, and put him to bed with a dry bandage on his leg.

"How'd y'all know how to do all that?" Apolina asked in awe. "That was crazy."

"We're soldiers," Nina told her. "Combat personnel have some sort of knowledge of field medicine. Never know when you'll need it. Some of us were even combat medics during a war."

Bible showered and came out of the bathroom wearing black sweatpants and a muscle shirt.

"Okay, baby," Yolie cooed at him. "My big daddy. Lookin' all good."

Bible was blushing and Uzenna even said so. "Boy if you was white, you'd be turning red. Stop doin' that to him, Yoyo. He can't take it."

The two women cooked fried chicken and Spanish rice while Nina spoke to Apolina in the living room. Bible sat next to Apolina.

"Joker has strip clubs all throughout Meth Alley States, right?" Apolina asked.

"Correct," Nina said, recording her as she spoke.

"Their organization, The One they call themselves, has brought over two hundred Albanian tattoo artists," Apolina expounded. "Men and women. Most are ex-felons, Albanian Mafia. She put them in all these tattoo shops they opened near Joker's clubs. In those shops they have sex slaves they use to manipulate the gangsters that -"

"Go back. *Sex slaves*?" Nina asked. "What gangsters?"

"They have a hook up with the Gulf Cartel and Tijuana Cartel," Apolina informed her. "Helena, Laila, and Nobi from the Tijuana Cartel – I don't know last names. Nico, Aurelio, Juan, and Kiko from the Gulf Cartel. Valoria is the NJË leader. She has a pipeline where girls come from Bangladesh, Ukraine, Romania, and Russia through Mexico to the United States."

"How are they getting in?" Nina probed.

"The shipping ports," Apolina replied. "I heard Honey complaining about how much it was costing them to pay off security officials at the L.A. and Long Beach ports nowadays."

Nina was shaking her head. "Security officials. Which – U.S. Customs are taking bribes from NJE, Ghostman, and Honey B... or the Tijuana and Gulf outfits?"

Apolina shrugged her shoulders. "They just got so comfortable talkin' around me... I'm just sayin' what I heard come out of their mouths."

"So, these gangsters..." Nina prodded her.

"Uh huh," Apolina nodded. "They have these lovely teen girls whose bodies they use as billboards to show off or advertise the tattoo shop they represent. They're only interested in MS-13, Bloods, Crips, Sureños, Latin Kings, Juggalos – gangs who rule the drug game and may wish to expand themselves into the meth game. They're in each tattoo shop and there's a fuckin' giant horde of them by now."

"You've seen them?" Nina asked.

Apolina shook her head. "Why you think I had to finally get out?"

Nina's eyes squinted. "Tell us."

"I started seein' two, three, four, and five of the pretty white teens come through the Winthrop mansion," Apolina started. "They were there as help I thought. They cleaned, served drinks, food, took care of the dogs… At first, I was relieved I didn't have to have sex every day with Ghostman because he's… he's a savage pervert. Honey B's sex is nice. But Ghostman would leave at night with a girl and he'd return alone the next day and she'd be gone."

"You mean one of the teen girls?" Nina clarified.

Apolina nodded. "They spoke English good enough and I was cool with them. You could tell that they were still innocent… still kids. Even though they were hardened by being sold off, stolen, snatched from home by these vile Albanian vagabonds. Anyway, I could hear Honey B yelling at him about how Valoria would catch wind of these girls comin' up missing. Then Honey B said something about how he was lucky that Joker knew nothin' about Cheekie, Esmeralda, and Daphne."

"*Cheekie?*" Uzenna said as she came out of the kitchen. She had plates of food which she sat down on the coffee table. "What about her?"

"She's dead," Apolina told her.

Cheekie had been one of the strippers that Uzenna had known for years and she'd brought her up to join the squad of dancers being put together to help expand the underground strip clubs. However, she had gotten expelled from the group for mouthing off at Red. Ghostman had volunteered to take her to the airport so she could return to Mississippi. But she had never returned because Ghostman had taken her, had sex with her, murdered her, and made her body disappear.

Apolina explained everything she'd heard about this to Uzenna.

"Cheekie's folks down there don't know nothin'," Uzenna said, shaking her head. "Ghostman… he been a cobra inside of the henhouse the whole time."

Apolina nodded. "He has this acute fascination with young women. I thought at first they just wanted them legal. Right at eighteen. But dig deeper in the digital files I sent you…and y'all see that he is totally *obsessed* with tender aged females and because of his money and access to the dark net, he has unlimited access to all of the illegal portals, anonymous software programs, Freenet, I2P, TOR, True-Crypt…and he ain't dumb. You won't trace none of it back to where he lives, does business or nothin'. I got lucky because we were in Mexico and he was online for hours at the hotel we were staying at… I waited for him and Honey B to go swimming and I retraced his internet history on the hotel computer and nearly lost it. I can't even talk about what I saw him lookin' at. Just view the sites."

"We need usernames, passwords, and -"

Apolina held her hand up. "He uses the same ones for everything. They're all in the files I sent over."

Everyone ate except Joker Red.

Uzenna went to wake him up but changed her mind. She was curling up alongside him when his cellphone vibrated. She saw that it was Don Frank Braga. She answered it and told him that Joker was okay but had been shot.

"Welcome to Chicago, sweetheart," Don Frank said. "I'm starting to hear a lot about the Albanian problem. I'm wondering if youse need my men to get involved."

"I don't know," Uzenna said. "Hold on."

She took the phone to Nina.

Nina greeted him, "Hello, Don Frank."

"The Albanians," Frank began. "They are not only stepping on EIE's toes but now they're stepping on mine. You tell Red to call me, okay?"

Nina looked at the phone with worry in her eyes now.

CHAPTER TWENTY-FIVE

Meth Man Ace
Campinas, Brazil

Meth Man Ace decided that a daytime move for Honey B's son would garner too many unseen or unexpected risks. So, in the wee hours of the next morning, he approached the Lexus SUV that was sitting in the driveway of the house that Bernyce Mejia lived in with Honey B's son, Victor. He walked past the truck and walked alongside the house.

There he found a glass door with a screen on it. Both of them were simple to pick and slide open. He stepped inside of the house and heard the buzz coming from the refrigerator motor. He walked past the kitchen and down a hallway that had four doors: one door was a bathroom. That was empty. The other was a closet where coats hung and the vacuum cleaner was stored.

To the left was the boy's bedroom. He slept on the top of the covers in a Spider-Man pajama suit. Meth Man left him alone for the time being. He entered Bernyce's room and immediately shot her with a tranquilizer gun. She jumped up and grabbed at the stabbing dart but it was way too later. The paralyzing effects of the drug acted very fast on humans. Then he doubled back and darted the boy.

"There's an alley out back," he whispered over the radio after tranquilizing the boy. *"Pull up out there to keep the neighbors blind, over."*

"Ten-four over and out," Alejandra came back.

He carried out Bernyce first and locked her in the trunk. Then he bundled up the kid in a blanket and put him in the rear of the vehicle. He jumped into the front passenger's seat and off they went.

They drove to the airport at the "Freight-Cargo Only" gate where Meth Man handed the official a black briefcase. The guard opened up the briefcase and inspected the stacks of US- currency inside of it. He opened up the automatic "stop" arm for them.

"The C-40 Clipper?" The official asked in Spanish.

Alejandra nodded. "Si, Senor."

"It's being refueled now," he said to them. "You only have twenty minutes before the camera are back on. Hurry."

They drove through and found the refueling hangar where their airplane was. Bonecrusher was standing outside of the aircraft with Lieutenant Gates smoking cigarettes.

"Hey, mufuckaz." Ace yelled out the window before hopping out of the car. He embraced the two men.

"What's good, nigga?" Bone boomed, standing back. "Getting all dark and shit, huh?"

"This Brazilian sun," Ace said.

"Nigga dressed like a Hawaiian an' shit." Boo said as he appeared and hugged Ace.

"Let's get these mufucka's outta the car before security come," Ace told them. "The nannie, y'all can dump out overseas for me."

"She dead?" Boo asked.

"I hit her wit that horse tranquilizer so she might as well be," Ace told them. "The kid I hit him wit a puppy dose."

They loaded the nanny and the kid on-board and secured them in a bedroom there. Once that was completed, everyone said their goodbyes.

"We only got a short time before the cameras come back up," Ace told them. "Y'all niggas be safe."

Alejandra and Ace drove straight back out of the airport's cargo-freight loading areas before they could be picked up on surveillance cameras. They returned to the nanny's residence, this time with all of Ace's wives there with them.

They packed up clothes and cosmetics belonging to Bernyce and Victor. They located her cellphone, laptop, and other electronics devices a person would not leave home without. They unplugged everything except the refrigerator and fish tank. If or when Honey B reported them missing, the police would come and Ace wanted it to look like they had left on vacation not went missing.

"I got the keys to the Lexus, Papi," Blanca told him around midday. "They don't have interior-exterior cameras, so…"

He was sitting behind the desktop computer writing an email out to Honey B about taking the boy to Buenos Aires for a few weeks since school was letting out for the summer. That they were driving down there to the beaches, amusement parks, and exotic animal's zoo.

"Don't say too much," Alejandra warned him as she read the email. "How'd you find her email password that quick anyway?"

Ace laughed and lifted up the desktop calendar. "Dumb ass got 'em all written down."

"Check her bank account," Blanca suggested. "She has to have a really nice stash."

He checked the balance of her account and it was close to $50,000 in there.

"I'm transferring it," he said. "We'll spend it when we get back to the States."

"You promised us a vacation," Bambina reminded him.

"We are," he told them. "Just not here."

"Not in this city or this country?" Natalya asked.

"This city," he said. "Did I tell y'all I met this amazin' woman we can all have a slice of?"

Bambina laughed. "You say it like she's bread or pie."

All the others laughed at that wry humor.

"Man, she's up a level like y'all," Ace assured them.

"We're in Brazil, Papi," Blanca said all sultry like. "We can test many pies, hm?"

"I'm hungry for these four first," he said.

He stood up and hugged Blanca and Bambina.

"Time to go," Natalya said. "We can play when we clear the job."

"I'll take the truck," Bambina said.

They packed all of the suitcases into the truck and headed out of the affluent neighborhood.

CHAPTER TWENTY-SIX

La Bella Marín
Campinas, Brazil

Yajaira Carmona Soto had decided to take the tall sexy, light skinned Black American up on his scorching hot offer to drop in on him and his four lovely Dominican wives at the upscale La Bella Marín hotel in Campinas. She had to be welcomed up first so the hotel desk clerk called Ace's Presidential Penthouse and it was Natalya who invited her up.

"Yajaira Carmona Soto!" Natalya yelled out to Ace who was upstairs on the SAT-phone with Joker Red.

"Hold on, Red," Ace said, walking over to the marble banister, looking down into the center of the suite. "What'd you say, mama?"

"Yajaira Carmona Soto is on her way up with someone else," Natalya told him, a bored look on her face.

"Oh, I forgot to tell y'all she has a really hot brother she's bringin' along," he said loud enough for all of his wives to hear.

"You *asshole*!" Bambina shouted and headed to the bathroom to shower and get herself all prettied up.

The rest of the women followed suit.

"So, they both bein' kept on the military base or what?" Ace continued his conversation with Joker. "Cuz I told Bone and nem to dump the nanny."

"They did," Joker confirmed. "Concrete bracelets and everything. She shrimp food."

Ace told Joker about the bogus email he'd sent to Honey B and how they'd packed the house up to throw cops off the scent in case they started a missing person investigation.

"Yeah, good move," Joker commended him. "They'll know I have the kid in the next ten days. I'll hold off."

Ace ended his call with Joker Red when the front doorbell rang and the Brazilian hotel maid answered it. He walked down the red carpeted staircase dressed in all white poolside sports style clothing by Gucci. It was hot in Campinas, so Ace was not going to overdress for nobody. However, when he saw Yajaira, he was knocked out because — although she was dressed in a simple ankle length tan summer dress with huge tropical flowers all over it – she looked dressed to kill.

"Olá," he smiled as he greeted her with two kisses, one on each cheek. "I got one word to describe you right now: pie."

"Huh?" She asked puzzled.

"Don't mess wit him, Mamacita," Alejandra waved him off dismissively. "Our Papi was just buggin'… talkin' about how you look and tasted and everything."

"He doesn't know all that," Yajaira said as Alejandra embraced her.

"This is my brother Pepe," Yajaira introduced a very good-looking man who was about six feet tall and had very black curly hair.

"*Mucho gusto*," Pepe said, shaking Ace's hand.

"Nice to meet you, too," Ace told him.

Pepe had a wedding band on, so he wasn't trying to conceal the fact that he had a wife. Ace thought he was cool. One by one, his wives showed up and they all seemed to like him.

"Ain't you taking her upstairs, Papi?" Blanca whispered to him.

"You rushin' me?" He whispered back. "This dude look like everybody sexiest soccer star all rolled up into one an' shit."

Blanca laughed so hard. "You so stupid. Go. She got eyes for you."

"Y'all don't want none of her?" He whispered once more. "I'll take some and throw her y'all way."

Natalya, sitting on the other side of him, heard. "I do but you need to go."

Ace didn't take her upstairs. "C'mon, mami. Let's walk."

Yajaira followed him down to the hotel's indoor swimming pool which was closed after midnight. But Ace slipped security $1000 to make sure that he was not disturbed.

"Let's go," he said to the South American beauty.

She followed him into the pool area but they walked past that.

"I don't have a swimsuit," Yajaira said to him.

"We can swim in our underwear."

"I'm not wearing any."

"Why? Too hot?"

She laughed as he led her down some stairs where there were private Jacuzzi rooms that hotel guests reserved for small groups or gathering. He chose one and they locked the door behind them. He started up the hot rock sauna and then the Jacuzzi filled up with hot water.

He embraced her and kissed her like he'd missed her. She leaned into his strength and passion for her. She had never been with an African American man before. In fact, he would only be her third man altogether. She'd had a boyfriend very briefly as a sophomore in high school. That was when she'd lost her virginity. But when she'd gone off to college and her high school flame had moved to Portugal with his family that relationship was over. She had met and married her current husband when she was nineteen and she'd dropped out of college to help him with his used car business. Once that was thriving, she'd enrolled into a flight attendant program for Azul Brazilian Airlines and that's how she'd established her independence from her husband.

She wasn't looking to be unfaithful. She loved her husband but they wanted different things. She'd wanted a baby but he told her to wait. That's why she'd finally decided to get her own career. Now at age 25, her husband was only having sex with her once or twice per month leaving her to her fingers, dildos, toys, and fantasies.

Then came Meth Man Ace and his confidence. His good looks. The open and "nasty" way he talked to her. NOBODY talked dirty to her like he did. Ace had had her charged from Costa Rica to Brazil and had her panties wet the entire time. What really had struck her was that he was married to four beautiful Dominican women – one he had a child with – and they had an "open" marriage. They were polyamorous.

"What are you thinkin' about?" he checked, breaking into her thoughts as he stood beside the Jacuzzi in all of his naked glory.

"You look so good and powerful," she told him with a proud smile and a lustful glint in her eye.

He stepped closer to her and hugged her again. "You are so very beautiful and sweet – my heart jumps when I smell you and look into your lovely face."

He helped her pull her long summer dress off over her head. *This girl, Yajaira,* Ace thought… she just had the most banging-est body he'd ever seen. Her 32D cup breasts were so perfect they sat upward and had dark brown nipples that stood up off of the areolae three quarters of an inch. He draped her dress over a massage table and walked slowly around her.

"Youse just a superbad bitch, from nose to them pretty ass toes," he stated as he pulled her backside close to him. "You think this little pussy…"

He used two fingers and slowly stroked her pussy seam, over her small, puckered asshole and stood in front of her. He ran the fingers under his nose, inhaling her heavenly aroma as she stared at him with her lips parted.

"You like that?" He asked her. "You like to see me smell your pretty pussy…and that perfect Brazilian butt you got?"

She slowly nodded. "You give me goosebumps…"

"Does your husband look at you like this?"

"No," she said in a small voice. "God no."

"But you're so beautiful… you're a privilege to him… a gift," Meth said as he hugged her.

She moaned when he brushed and thrust his big hard dick up against her mound.

"Uhhmmm, Ace. My legs are wobbly." She moaned and held onto him, squeezing his full fleshy and firm back and ass cheeks.

He took her over to the Jacuzzi and sat her on the side of it where it was cushioned all around. He waded a little bit down into the warm water and encircled his muscular arms around her slender waist.

"You ever cheat on your husband before?" He asked as they passionately French kissed and his big hands were all over her breasts, pinching her nipples.

She shook her head. "No… I'm sorry but-"

"Baby, no sorry. That nigga don't be worshipping you like a goddess or queen. You a fuckin' nine plus one day. You saw my wives, right? All dimes. Happy ones. I encourage them to be themselves. Look at you. Open up, baby. Lemme see that hole wit all the sweet juice comin' out of it."

She let him place her feet up on his shoulders and she spread open her light brown Brazilian thighs. She kept it completely bald waxed. Her labia lay open with two swollen petals at the sides and the dimmed lights inside of the Jacuzzi room reflected off of the hot pinkness inside.

He put his arms around her ass and squeezed. "Baby, if your husband ain't between these beautiful legs, down on his knees like this, putting his lips, tongue, and nose all up in this lovely pussy you have… smelling you and swallowing each drop of your honey…then he ain't worshipping you. Fuck him, I'll do it. Mmmm, so good. I'll do it…"

Her clit was erect, big, protruding, but he kissed and teased it. He pushed her back some so he could also tongue her wet asshole. She laid all the way back on the deck, he had her feet up on the cushioned edge as he ate and worshipped her. She reached down, suddenly screaming out in orgasm.

"Ooooooooooeeeee. Ooooooooeeeee. Oh. My God." She fell to pieces as he sucked her clit and massaged her g-spot at the same time. She loved what he was doing to her. The pleasure was like needles pricking her over every inch of her body. "Ace."

"Where – uh, where da fuck yo little ass goin'?" He asked as his tongue thrashed her clit in insane circular motions. She was whipping her ass around and around and around, pushing her slice into his mouth one minute but then the next minute she was trying to back away when the mini orgasms became bigger ones. That's one thing the lovely Yajaira could do – she could cum with the most syrupy bursts of pussy cream Ace had ever tasted.

"I can't take no more," she whined and curled up in a ball on the deck, holding her hand over her pussy. "No more," she panted. "Wait…"

Ace smiled. *Little bitch ain't used to bussin' and squirtin' like that.* "C'mere, then, mami."

She looked up at him and sat on his lap with her face in his neck. "You made it feel too good. I'm – I just couldn't take it."

He kissed her tenderly. Sweetly. Gently. He popped a bottle of chilled Ace of Spades and poured them both a glassful. He felt her left hand work its way down his hairy chest and across his washboard abs.

"Let's go over there," she suggested to him. By this time, the room was nice and steamed up. They took clean beach towels and laid them across the large, cushioned sofa next to the massage table. Ace poured a scoop of water over the stones.

She had him sit back on the sofa and she got down on her knees. "My turn to worship you like the King you are. I'm so grateful to the pleasure you've brought me that I'm feeling something overwhelming in my soul about you that I probably shouldn't feel because I have a husband…and you have wives."

She kissed him all over his big dickhead and felt his precum wetting her lips. She licked it and moaned. She gently squeezed his huge sack as she licked up one side of his oversized shaft and then the other.

"God you are so big." She said in wide eyed wonder. She laughed and stood up. She went to the steel water pan and scooped some of it up and poured the warm liquid over his fat dick. "I am not leaving until you get at least half of it in me."

She resumed sucking the fully soaked lumber, taking enough of it into her mouth to make him start moaning and fucking up and down, in and out of her mouth.

"Make sure you relax your throat, Mami, and don't think about it when it makes you gag," he coached her. She closed those coffee brown eyes and did as he said. "It's okay…"

She took it out to gag a few times but she went right back to it with those gag tears and all falling from her eyes. No girl ever did that with him. Usually, they would wipe their eyes and stop or at least pause to catch their breath. But Yajaira was a different breed. She was also so sex-deprived she wanted and needed the feel and taste of a man all over her body, in her mouth, and everywhere else.

She started to take more and more of that huge brown dick deeper into her face and Ace started to fuck her throat more confidently. "Oooh, yeah, Brazilian Girl, suck that big black dick. Eat my dick down your throat, girl. Fuck your face with it."

His dirty talk spurred her on. Her throat was open so wide now that every time he thrusted inwards his balls would hit her chin. That excited her so much that she started face-fucking him even faster. She had caught on to what an awesome deep throat was. Her saliva was flowing out real good, too, cascading and soaking her hands and his balls.

"Uhh, ooh, mami! Fuckin' swallow that fuckin' cum!" He cried as he gushed warm splashes of his seed all down her throat. "That's right, baby. Now rub that cum juice all over that lovely face."

She loved what he was commanding her to do. She took his semi-hard anaconda and used it to smear the semen left over all over her face. She took in his taste, the smell of warm, fresh semen, and it made her horny as fuck.

They got back into the Jacuzzi for a few minutes.

"I never did that." She said. "I've never swallowed it or took it in my throat."

"I know but you did it for me and that's because I'm makin' you *mine*," Ace said while carrying her back out of the water and back over to the outdoor sofa. "You kinda already know that, dontcha?"

She nodded. "I said it – that I was feelin' something maybe I shouldn't…"

"Feel it," he urged her. "Cuz you makin' me yours, too. Ain't that why you came to La Bella Marín tonight? Do you want one fantastic moment you can't have again?"

"No. I want you." She assured him.

"This won't be the end then, I swear to you, okay?" He said as he laid her out on the sofa and opened her legs wide.

"My pussy is too small for that," she said afraid. He loved her accent so much.

He started to kiss her and felt himself harden like steel. "We have all night if we want. My wives won't care."

She giggled and suckled on his neck as he fit the large bulbous head of his meat into her wet, dripping cavern. He felt her clamping down and releasing with her young vagina muscles.

"What do you think they're doin' right now?" She asked him.

A girl never asked him that before. "Natalya is most aggressive sexually. But none of them are selfish. If he can go marathon then he could be fucking one at a time. Right now, he prolly makin' slow love to Blanca. To really get what they want outta him, they'll eat him like vampires for two or three days."

Her hips were swiveling as he was sinking an inch at a time into her.

"You are so tight." He whispered. "But so fuckin' good. Please baby, stop movin'. You gonna make me fuckin' cum."

They looked each other in the eyes and wiped the dripping sweat the steam was causing off of each other. He licked her neck all over and sucked each ear. He got his dick control back and started to fuck her again, very slowly.

"Baby, Mami… look dead at me," he told her as she turned her head and closed eyes.

"Don't put no more in," she stated, out of breath. "It won't-" he was whimpering.

"Relax everything," he coached her. "Didn't I say I was makin' you mine?"

"Si. Yes, Papi," she nodded. "You did."

"Then concentrate," he ordered her. "Relax everything. Your belly, your chest, breath normally, even your little asshole, and every muscle you got. Don't brace yourself for pain. Open yourself for yourself, for your new man to be inside of his pussy. That's right, I see the vein in your neck disappear."

He kissed her shoulders and squeezed her 32D breasts. They kissed like honeymooners in heat. She started doing that swiveling thing with her hips again, her juices washing over his big dick like a caddy in a car wash. The second she went into one of her mini-orgasmic spasms he thrust his entire bone deep up inside of her belly. It's like he had to just rip through a second cherry.

"Ace. Oh my God… Ace!" she screamed.

"That's it, Mamacita. Cum all over that black cucumber. We did it, Mami. We bust open a second pussy in there. Now put that sexy phat ass up in my face."

She turned over, clitoris visible, pussy lips pulsating like crazy. He made her put one foot on the ground and her right knee in the sofa with her ass bussed wide open. First things first, he put his face down in it and sniffed. But she only smelled like the steam droplets and her own leaking pussy cream. He kissed her asshole.

"You smell too clean right now, Mami," he whispered as he lined his hard dick up with her open pink hole. "I need some sweat on it or somethin'."

She giggled. "You are so wickedly dirty and nasty, Papi," she loved it.

He was ruthless this time. He thrust every inch of his lumber all the way inside of her, nearly knocking her breath away. He grabbed her light brown booty and started out with a slow deliberate pounding of her light brown colored ass.

He rubbed her sweaty back and got ahold of a handful of her hair.

"That's, umm. Papi, fuck me." She pushed him on. "I can feel you in my stomach. You took all this pussy, Papi. I never knew so much dick could go in me." She wanted to be dog fucked. "Papi go – fuck me like a whore. *Your* whore."

He pulled her hair hard as fuck. He didn't mean it, he was just getting carried away at how tight and wet her pussy was. Looking at her tiny asshole and how her little pussy looked taking such a huge dick was incredible. His big balls were slapping her clitoris and that made her start playing with her own clit as he hammered her to oblivion. He beat that pussy in like crazy.

"Can't stop it. Yajaira…Ooouuu, fuck this pussy mad good."

"Don't…um…shit." She had just remembered that they were fucking unprotected. She was trying to tell him not to cum inside of her. But it would feel so good if he did. "I'm not on birth control or – ohh."

She laid flat on the sofa, legs wide as he slammed serious pipe down deep into her and bit her neck and licked her lips as he lost control.

"I'm bussin' all up in that pussy, Mami. I'm Cuuuuummmmmiii-innngggg! Oh, fuck… I'm cummin' so much."

She came all over his pole right along with him and all but fainted. She had never had so many orgasms and never had she felt such a cosmic connection to a man before. He laid out on the floor and she laid next to him.

"Ace?" she said.

"Yeah, Mami."

"I really need you in my life."

He paused. "Get your passport for the U.S. all clear."

"It is."

"We got a long way to go to truly know each other," he said. "But… I know you another man's wife. So, it's gonna bum me out to know you so many miles away."

There was a really long pause. She was thinking. "What if I left him… I mean we are more like roommates now than anything so what if?"

"Lemme tell you about me," he started. "I was in the U.S. Army – a combat medic. I studied chemistry in college. I belong to a private military company. We are rogue soldiers, mercenaries, highly trained killers. We joined our leader and started up a major national methamphetamine distribution network in the United States and now internationally over the Dark Net. But the government intervened and made us a deal: help them on certain missions, using some of our own funds. Or they could send us all to prison for previous crimes. That's about as much as I can tell you right now."

She snuggled closer to him. "I knew you were some kind of gangster, a mafia, or something."

"Keep my secrets," he warned her.

"I vow it," she said. "So where in the U.S. do you live? In New York City?"

"I'm from New York but we were in Chicago for a couple of years. But I now have land in Jasper, Florida." He paused for a moment. "Our primary operation center is being moved. That's to Florida… I can use a girl like you."

"Well," she said. "Look for me when I arrive in Florida."

CHAPTER TWENTY-SEVEN

Young Army Members Smoke, Rome, and Brook were standing in the foyer with their mother Natasha Catherine Hodges who was still showing her excitement at seeing her sons again. Bonecrusher had picked her up from the airport with Casci Caliendo along for the drive and brought her back to the West Palm Beach estate.

Joker heard all the noise and knew it was his older sister arriving from the airport. He was already on the first floor in the children's game room watching them pay more attention to their electronic devices than to him. Even when he tried to ask for kisses from his daughters they'd ignore him.

"Ayo girl." Joker boomed as he scooped the 5 feet 8-inch 190-pound woman off of her feet. "You trimmin' up?"

She kissed her brother and hugged him. "Hell yes. It's summer almost. I ride my bike everywhere now. I cut off twenty pounds already no diet, just bike riding and pole dancing classes."

He looked at her. "You got a man now?"

"Yeah, ma, what the fuck?" Smoke asked. "Pole dancing? That's TMI any way you put it."

Brook laughed. "That's like tellin' us you switched from an applicator to a pad."

"Ha… all y'all sound dumb," the green-eyed brown skinned woman said. "Don't make me cuss y'all asses out. Pole dancing is an exercise many women do with no man or relationship in sight."

"You look real good, sis," Joker told her.

Natasha indicated her sons. "You didn't lie. They look like men now."

"They're a private unit inside of my Private Military Corporation (PMC)," Joker explained. "They've trained well but not enough to be sent to Africa or the Middle East on high stakes missions to kidnap, assassinate, or bomb anything. I told you I got 'em."

Smoke, Rome, and Brook took off.

Joker's wives all came out to greet Natasha. Everyone was at the mansion. The entire EIE Army was called in from the Meth Alley strip clubs and their positions were all switched with that of legitimate security services personnel from local companies in those cities.

Natasha entered the children's game room. She hugged and kissed on all of her nieces and nephews before eyeing Rose Rice Donohue, Kalani Muhammad, and Ariel Montoya. "Who are these beautiful young ladies?" Natasha inquired.

"Hey, girls," Joker said and introduced Natasha. "This is my sister, Tasha."

"Miss Tasha to y'all," she corrected them.

There were several nannies in the room he introduced her to as well. "My babies have computers for toys and they think it's really toys but they're in school all day," Joker laughed.

Natasha went upstairs with Joker where she was given her own room. "You paid for this place?"

"Leasing temporarily until our houses are built," he told her. "We're building an entire community of upscale houses each mom will move into with my kids. A very secure gated community."

"Why'd you rush me down here, J.R? What's goin' on?" She wanted to know.

"Your life's in danger," Joker warned her. "I got O'Mira comin' down with her kids. Anyone I care about I'm bringin' here until this war is over."

"War?" Natasha stated. "That gots nothin' to do with Natasha Catherine Hodges. I have a damned good job with Verizon, a nice apartment…"

Joker looked at her. "C'mere."

She followed him into the master bedroom where he opened up a secret room behind a wall bookshelf. He opened up the vault and she walked in.

"Oh my God, Joker!" She exclaimed as she looked all around the vault. On each shelf heaped high were stacks of cash in every conceivable denomination. "Is it all real?"

"What?" He shot back. "I ain't even answering that. Point is you don't ever have to worry about money again. You wanna earn your keep, work for EIE, Inc. at our Florida Central Intelligence Network or CIN. What do you make at Verizon?"

"Thirty-nine grand," she said. "What is CIN?"

"It tracks every employee that works for me," he educated her. "What they're doing, who they're calling or texting. You know the doorbell camera technology?"

She nodded.

"I can see everything," he told her. "We did use hundreds of strippers to operate about twenty-five underground clubs all throughout the Meth Alley States. Once the CIA got interested in EIE, we moved into legitimate, licensed clubs in those same cities and state. We paid for all of the FBI's top spy cameras, bugs, and equipment to be installed everywhere. Even in the apartments I let the girls and employees live in. See this?"

He showed her the fancy cellular phone he had.

"It looks expensive," she said.

"NSA created it," he mentioned. "It's an encrypted company phone. Everyone must have one. It has every protection a criminal can think of or a military corporation who wants to guard secrets. But CIN can analyze and retrieve all data from it."

"It's not that encrypted then," she said, thumbing through some of the cash.

"Maaan…we watchin' everybody," he said. "But I can use you at CIN where your salary will be thirty grand more – not to mention every other perk. I'll give you a car, a nice place to call your own, and Leah will be your supervisor over there."

"My apartment. I need all my stuff," she said.

He shook his head. "Gimme the keys and I'll have it all professional boxed, wrapped, loaded, and shipped."

"What's really goin' on, Jay? Huh? You scratchin' all over the surface."

"That fuckin' nigga Ghostman done got tangled up with this ruthless Spanish bitch who got ties with Mexican Drug Cartels," he informed her. "They teamed up wit the Albanian Mob and tried to assassinate me. I took out two of them in a car chase that nearly killed me and then like six more while rescuin' a girl of mine that had been spying on them for me. Recently, we found out where Honey B was hiding her son. Brazil. Now we're holding him."

"Y'all kidnapped a boy?"

"He's safe but he's a valuable asset in the war," Joker explained. "That's why you're here."

He handed her a stack of cash and they walked out of the vault, locked it, and sat down on the Eames chairs near the balcony windows.

"You'll train with O'Mira," he continued on. "She runs a very lucrative operation for me in New York's TPP locations. Those locations are about to move down here. As for the rest of our family… Imma move them into a forty-room Colonial in Camden County, Georgia. Even parts of the family I can care less for. We'll give 'em cars, trucks, the deed to the house, and money to get started. Then my part is done."

They went back into the kids' game room but the nannies had taken them outside to get some sun. Only Uzenna, Coral, Ashley, Eden,

Valerie, Iani, Brittani, and Leah remained in there to clean up and disinfect the room and equipment the children had used.

Joker and Natasha helped them out.

"So you made it, brother," Natasha stated. "No more armored cars and banks... or kingpins. But... besides the mansions, lavish ladies, and the *Game of Thrones* military you lead – I just see bigger worries. Then this crystal meth empire. When will you ever sleep? You'll have no peace."

He nodded. "I do a lot of thinkin' and there's a reason I even made the CIA-DOD deal."

Some of his men entered the room just to hang around and listen. Casci, Breach, Bible, Boo, Knox, and others.

"Yeah," Natasha said. "Why'd you get in bed wit the CIA?"

"It cleared all of our names from all known and unknown crimes first off," Joker said, sitting down on the end of one of the four sofas in the large room. "That's here, on American soil and overseas. No prison worries."

More of his army entered and sat around.

"The government alliance gives many of us- even my wives- a chance to wash away all our past sins," Joker told his sister. "We taking on noble missions. Those three young girls you met – Rose Rice Donohue, Ariel, and Kalani? We rescued them from Albanian sex traffickers in Vegas."

"Is that white girl the one from the news?" Natasha suddenly realized. "No!" She gasped.

Joker nodded. "That's her. Her mom and dad came here with the FBI's knowledge and agreed to let her stay until we neutralize the Albanians."

"You mean kill," Natasha clarified.

Joker shrugged. "There's some ugly shit goin' on in America. If killaz can roam in secret, then the only way to stop them is with a secret army of killaz." The meth? I don't have my heart in it like I once did, but part of the deal was to fund EIE by any means necessary. Since these pipe suckin', needle pokin' junkies are weak then let 'em gorge on the meth. The way I see it I'm doin' good wit the money."

"Like Robin Hood?" Natasha offered.

Joker shook his head. "Nah, sis. Robin Hood stole from the rich and gave to the poor. What EIE, Inc. is doin' is takin' from the weak to save those with the potential to be strong. I hate sex traffickers, slave masters, and lowdown dirty cockroach mufuckaz…"

"Boss, when we having this meetin'?" Bible inquired.

Joker looked at his watch. "Don Frank, Vinnie, and some ethers still gotta fly in. Our Ghostman, Honey B, Albanian – and any other problem – all about to be settled. Anybody hungry? I'm told they got giant lobsters in there cooking."

They all went to enjoy the King's Feast.

CHAPTER TWENTY-EIGHT

Don Frank Braga
West Palm Beach

Don Frank Braga and his underboss (and younger brother) Vinnie "The Butcher" arrived in Florida as promised and were accompanied by a ten-man entourage. They were treated as special guests of Joker Red's and met at the airport by Joker Red himself.

"Fuck the traffic, we have helicopter clearance," Joker told them and escorted the dozen men to where two helicopters were waiting for them.

They were flown to West Palm Beach heliport and picked up by waiting stretch Mercedes and Hummer limousines. Not even five minutes away from the Hodges Estate was a fabulous property with an 8.7-million-dollar price tag. It was a beautiful mansion that had seven bedrooms, ten bathrooms, thirty rooms altogether. The place was amazing.

"It has two cottages with eight more bedrooms so that's more than enough bed space," Joker said as they entered the main house. "There's a staff that came with the house, too. Wanna meet 'em?"

Big Frank spread his hands out. "Sure, where are they?"

"Out back," Joker pointed to the expansive swimming pool and view of the beaches.

"Joker, you son of a-" Vinnie laughed.

There had to be at least thirty near naked women out there. Some were in the swimming pool while others were laid out in the sun tanning.

"Your guests are here, ladies." Joker told the women. The girls all came up to the Mafia bosses and said hello. The women helped carry all of the men's luggage in and helped them to where they would be sleeping.

"Hey, Vin," Joker called to him. Vinnie was in the room next to Don Frank's.

Inside of that room was a very large traveling trunk. Vinnie took the key Joker gave him to open it, which he did right away.

"Beautiful," Don Frank nodded as he saw all of the weapons.

"I know y'all feel naked because you can't carry on planes so…" Joker trailed off.

"Thank you," Vinnie said as he put on a shoulder holster and holstered two Glocks.

"Citra." Joker yelled and in came a beautiful raven-haired girl with green eyes. "She's from Afghanistan. She had come over with all the refugees. She's twenty, she speaks very good English, and of all things she's a Christian stripper."

"You're a Christian stripper?" Vinnie repeated.

"He meant a stripper who is Christian," Citra corrected with a smile and playfully poking her tongue out at Joker. "Everyone automatically thinks because I'm from Afghanistan that we are all Muslim. That is not true. Five to ten percent of us are Christian and heavily persecuted by Taliban."

"Okay," Vinnie said, loving her already. "I'm in love."

She smiled prettily.

"Well," Joker started. "Love's a good start. But this one wants college and much more."

Joker reached into the trunk, removed a duffel bag, and opened it up. "The girls will love you more with some of this."

Don Frank Braga laughed, staring at the cash.

"Anyway," Joker said. "Citra here is number one over these girls. She knows the house, the keys, the alarm codes, and there's several cars outside for your use. Literally five minutes from here is my place. Citra will get you there. This house is just extra bed space."

$\sim$

The West Palm Beach Estate

JOKER RETURNED TO HIS OWN WEST PALM BEACH ESTATE AND PULLED Leah to the side. There was obviously an impromptu pool party put together by Uzenna to entertain everyone because so many EIE members and associates were rolling into town.

"What's up, Daddy?" Leah asked as they stood next to the wall-mounted fish tank that covered the entire hallway wall leading into the library downstairs. Anyone who walked into the house had to marvel at the architectural genius that went into constructing the fish tank which was filled with beautiful black tipped reef sharks and lionfish. "I think one of the sharks is pregnant."

He looked at the tank as the sharks stalked to and from through their environment.

"Who's here so far?" He asked her.

They looked out of the large arching windows, in the dining room, out into the backyard. Leah reported to him that she did not know if everybody that he needed to be there had arrived.

"I'll get a look," he told her. "But Imma need a checklist to see who hasn't made it."

As he walked around greeting and showing love to his peoples he also checked them off the list he had on the iPad Leah had handed off to him. One of his main men from the Brooklyn streets was there.

"Boo, what up, nigga?" Joker said, handshake hugging him.

The dark-skinned young man with waves in his hair and big eyes was all smiles. He was a former Army Ranger sniper and combat veteran. He was with his wife, a very pretty woman, a bit plump around the middle but a looker nonetheless. She was Haitian and Dominican.

"You remember Satzi," Boo said.

"How can I forget? She turned me down in public school, junior high, and by high school, I stopped tryin'." Joker hugged her and kissed her cheek. "Hey, Satzi."

"Hello," she returned. They spoke for several minutes before Joker moved on. He noticed Bonecrusher, Hard Knox, Divine, Meth Man Ace, and his four wives all huddled together on the back deck drinking beers. Further down—laying out on poolside lounge chairs—were Broliks, Bushwacker, Breach, Devastator, Starscream, and-Transformer- Ironhide.

There was a barbeque pit which was stone-crafted on the outskirts of the swimming pool area. Joker saw pilots of EIE—Rebel One, Blackbird, and Darkstar—being handed plates with fresh ribs hot off the grill. He saw Natasha at the bar having a drink with Lieutenant Sampson Gates. Joker stood off and observed from a distance how they both were acting. She was laughing at his jokes, flirting with him.

Joker was approached by Apolina, Yolie Santana, Carla De Leon, and Isabella Caronna. He embraced Apolina first and whispered into her ear. "Can I trust you?" He asked her.

"C'mon, Red," she said, glaring at him. "Haven't I proved my fuckin' self enough amongst all these EIE bitches?"

"Not getting high, you didn't," he told her. "I don't care about a perk or zany to take the edge off but if you takin' dat shit constantly then you get in rehab. You can't be no zombie on this level up here wit us."

"*Lo prometo*, I won't let you down," she swore.

He nodded. "Aight, mami. Go enjoy da party."

"I need to show you a video I found in one of Ghostman's emails," she said.

"Later," he said, looking at Carla and Isabella who were like family to the missing Italian mistress of Vinnie Braga. "Tell them straight out, Apple."

He sometimes called Apolina "Apple" because it sounded good.

"Tell us what?" Carla asked.

Isabella felt a tightness form inside of the pit of her stomach.

"Jessika was raped and killed by Ghostman," Apolina said straight-forwardly but there was a noticeable degree of compassion in her voice.

"Where's her body so we can send her home to be buried?" Isabella asked with a deep sadness in her Italian-accented voice.

"Carla Dee and Isabella, listen to me," Joker urged them with a built-up rumbling anger in his voice. "Go wit Apple. She's gonna explain a lot of shit them snakes have been doing for months behind my back. But somethin' real catastrophic is about to go down and we'll all have vengeance. We may not have Cheekie, Esmeralda, Daphne Jessoms, Jessika, and whoever else that murderin' Bushwacker raped and buried…"

Apolina got the point. She walked off with the Italian women.

"Yolie, what's good?" He greeted her.

"I was wondering," she stated with a slight tease.

"Wondering what?"

"When we get married, will you be there?" She blurted.

Joker noticed an entire gang of new faces enter the backyard and many EIE Army members were embracing them. One of those "new" faces was his homie Junga who was fresh home from prison after winning his appeal.

Junga hugged Brittani who Joker had given permission to fuck on one occasion. But that was a long time ago; at least two years-plus, when Joker had started to first move paper narco products into the prisons using the U.S. Mail system. However, that was a one-time thing and Joker would have to make that clear.

"Damn, right Imma be there," Joker looked at her like she'd bumped her head or something. "That's my friend."

"I'm pregnant," Yolie admitted.

Joker grinned. "That's good news, Yolie."

She had a long face.

Joker shook his head like he knew something bad was coming. "What is it, Yoyo?"

She took a deep breath. "I have regular high-end clients and a rich white married couple came to see me at your new club in Gary, Indiana."

"Clapperz Strip Club, go on," he told her.

"We had a private room for the wife- it was her birthday," Yolie explained. "They paid really, really good so me and her was freakin' out ass naked. She never had her pussy ate by a woman so I went in on her. Her husband was supposed to just watch. But he wraps it up and fucks me from the back. I was not comfortable with it because I told Bible I'd stop hustlin' like that."

"Okay…so dude was wrapped up?" Joker wanted to know.

"Yeah, I mean no," she jumbled up her words. "He was but like I said, I was uncomfortable so I went dry on him. He pulls the fuckin' condom off and finished inside of me. So I'm mad afraid of the dates."

"The person you need to talk to is Bible," Joker advised her. "Be straight up. We all know those private rooms. Shit happens when the champagne flows in there. Don't put it off. Talk to him now."

He watched her walk away and his eyes went back to Junga who was still talking to Brittani, so Joker headed in that direction.

CHAPTER TWENTY-NINE

The West Palm Beach Estate
West Palm Beach, FL

Benjamin "Junga" Tines had been the leader of the Rollin' 60's Crips up in Elmira Correctional Facility. Joker had vowed to plug in with him after Joker went home. When Joker had sent Uzenna, Brittani, Coral, and Iani to visit him and smuggle in narcotics to get the ball rolling on the "prison plan," Joker had given Brittani the green light to make a play on him sexually. Afterall, at that time, he'd been in prison for ten years.

Brittani had did him a favor and even as Joker was approaching, Junga had already gotten the picture. Joker embraced him.

"Glad you could make it," Joker told him. "When you get out?"

"Two days ago," Junga told him. "I knew you had a plane ticket waiting for me, so I said fuck New York. Ayo. Who da fuck got the canary yellow Maybach outside though?"

"I think that's Meth's shit," Joker guessed. "Hey Meth."

Meth Man excused himself from a group he was talking to and walked over to the frosted glass topped, wrought iron frame, poolside tables that Brittani and a few other of his wives were seated at.

"What up wit it, cuz?" Meth inquired as he held a lit blunt in his left hand.

"This Junga," Joker introduced the two. "Junga helped us get this whole thing started when he—"

"Oh, you was the cat in El Mira," Meth quickly realized, hand-shake-hugging Junga. "Welcome home, nigga."

Junga nodded, making a behind-the-shoulder thumb gesture. "That yellow Maybach you, kid?"

"Sixty of 'em in the world special edition," Meth said nodding. "I'm Ace."

"C'mon, Junga." Joker walked inside of the house and saw Don Braga, Vinnie, their muscle, and nearly all of the new EIE dancers, Joker greeted them and led Junga into the home library- office. "Lemme be straight witchu, son. Brittani, like all of my wives, are off-limits. What happened years ago wit you and Brittani, I gave you that… as a one-time gift."

"Aiight, aiight, don't go crazy on me, son," Junga said. "I been in jail forever and whoever a familiar face and we good wit each other, Imma show my teeth, to. I wouldn't do nothin' to diss you, homie."

"Nor I you." Joker reached across the desk and banged hands hard with him. "Good to see you home. What's your plan?"

Junga shook his head. "I owe you a lot, man. Whatchu need?"

"You still got that Crip Army connect?"

Junga smiled. "Yeah."

"You got cash stashed?"

Junga nodded again. "Came home wit seventy thousand. My baby moms ran through the rest."

Joker sucked his teeth. "She had your shorties for thirteen years. Anyway, Imma need all y'all to be trained militarily. I have a clandes-tine army base in the Dakotas."

Junga had a funny look on his face.

"Not right now but you and whoever you wanna bring into EIE… we on some different shit. Y'all gotta be trained because EIE, Inc. is a legit private military corporation now. We literally own Meth Valley USA and I got soldiers out there killin' comp and opps all the time to protect it. We in a war right now and y'all need to know more than how to fire an AR or AK or attach a Glock switch. We're fightin' the Albanians."

Junga nodded. "Okay. So, what now?"

"I have twenty plus strip clubs in Meth Alley," Joker revealed. "Clapperz Strip Clubs."

"Like booty clappin'?"

"Exactly," Joker responded. "First, move your army down here and we'll get you all apartments. Miami, Orlando, Jacksonville, Atlanta, New Jersey, New York, I want y'all to scout out the best locations. The other job I got, I need y'all to assist with the narco-paper operation. That's plenty of work."

"Findin' locations… stampin' some envelopes," Junga feigned like he was weighing the two with both of his big hands. "Sounds like you need a real estate agent and another secretary."

Joker laughed. "Son, you just got home. Ease back into life outside. Two grand a week to you, a grand a week to your associates."

Junga stood up and shook Joker's hand. "Well, sir, you just hired yourself a real estate agent and a secretary."

"Funny, nigga." Joker placed two glasses on the desk and poured two shots of his $5000-a-bottle Courvoisier. He reached into the desk and pulled out a bank bag. "Keep receipts of all transactions, expenses, everything. You get some pussy yet, nigga?"

Junga shook his head.

Joker texted Carla and Isabella. Several minutes later they entered the office-library.

"This is Junga," Joker introduced them. "Why don't y'all go on into Miami and have a good time? Stay all night at the Copacabana. Their penthouses are unbelievable."

"Okay," Isabella said, smiling at Junga.

"He hasn't had a woman in thirteen years," Joker told them.

"Shit," Carla muttered, eyeing him. "We got this, J.R."

Joker handed her the entire roll of cash he had on him, which was more than enough to cover the Copacabana. Joker exited the office after them.

CHAPTER THIRTY

"The Orgy"
West Palm Beach Estate

Leah scanned the entire guest list on the desk top computer the next day and whispered to herself, "That's everybody. Thank God."

She printed it off and brought it to Joker who was just getting up. He sat on the side of the gigantic new Ultra bed and watched as Leah sauntered into the room wearing pink cutoffs and a halter top with a dozen different splotchy designs on it. She also wore cute pink Nike thongs on her feet.

"Baby, I swear you make a nigga have a foot fetish wit them pretty ass toes," he said as she handed him the paper. "Get on the bed, put 'em in my lap. Do they stink?"

She giggled and slapped the back of his head. "Nuttin' on me stinks. I keep it all one hundred percent. See?"

He sniffed her toes. "They do smell good. Like the rest of you. What's this?"

"Everybody's in town," she told him. "Your precious checklist," she said sarcastically.

"You gon' make me fuck you up," he said, plucking for her ear but he missed. "Talkin' shit…"

He examined all the names on the list:

-Boo
-Hard Knox
-Meth Man Ace
-Breach
-Caesar
-Blackout
-Devastator
-Ironhide
-Blackbird
-Natasha
-Apolina
-Carla
-Junga
-Casci/Columbiana
-Nina Overstreet
-Maxine Crawford
-String Bean (EIE)
-Blink (EIE)
-Creeper (EIE)
-Goofy (EIE)
-Showtime (EIE)
-Alvin Zalamea (EIE)
-Big Zeus
-Brook (Y.A.)
-Jimmie (Y.A.)
-Bonecrusher
-Divine
-Bushwacker
-Goliath
-Bible
-Barricade
-Starscream

-Rebel One
-Darkstar
-Lt. Gates, S.
- Yolie
-Isabella
-Brolik's
-Nyomi Malik
-Bryson Bailey
-Vinnie Braga
-Venom (EIE)
-Spanky (EIE)
-Boogeyman (EIE)
-Mambo (EIE)
-Chopper (EIE)
-Rome (Y.A.)
-Smoke (Y.A.)
-Mojo (Y.A.)
-Blood Money (Y.A.)
-Big Crip (Y.A.)
-Hop (Y.A.)
-Grim (Y.A.)
-Budda Clips (Y.A.)
-Blue (Y.A.)
-Crime (Y.A.)
-Streetlyfe (Y.A.)
-Badman (Y.A.)
-Tip Toe (Y.A.)
-Boom (Y.A.)
-Rampage (Y.A.)
-Cocaine (Y.A.)

"You got a lot of new girls, too," Leah said as Eden woke up and wrapped her arms around his mid-section. "Good morning, Edie. I love you, bae."

Eden smiled. He looked behind him. "When'd all y'all come in here anyway?"

All of his wives were comfortably asleep in the massive bed. There was no sex last night. They'd just all crashed with Joker.

"I love all of y'all," Joker told them. When they wouldn't stir Joker said, "Yeah, Uzenna nem been recruitin' hard."

"You don't see nuttin' you like?" Leah queried. "That Polynesian girl Zaza is somethin'."

Joker shrugged. "I ain't feelin' nothin' but the eight beautiful wives I have. I have the world just with you alone with Edie alone. But I get eight, with nine beautiful children – five sons, four daughters. Now you, Edie, China, and Uzenna are pregnant once more? We gonna have the biggest family in America."

"We wasn't even tryin' this time," Eden finally spoke.

There was a light tap on the door.

"Yep." Leah called out.

Apolina walked in wearing an extremely sexy and revealing micro bikini, looking like she came out of the Latin Sports Illustrated swimsuit issue magazine. She thrusted an encrypted cellphone into Joker's hand declaring: "First, it was Honey B and now Ghost yellin' and threating about her missing son."

"What da fuck you want, dirtbag nigga?" Joker said as calmly as he could.

"I want my fuckin' son, Joker!" He could hear Honey B shouting in the background.

Joker hung the phone up. "Apple, don't answer no more calls from any of 'em. The kid is how we're gonna control life and death for both of them. You see how I got everybody here under heavy protection. Follow my lead."

"Just keep her phone, Daddy," Eden suggested.

"Give her a new phone, Lee," Joker stated as he turned around and kissed her with mad passion.

"I have my whole life in that phone." Apolina said to Leah as she watched Eden and Joker kiss as if they were about to fuck for the first time ever. He effortlessly lifted Eden into his arms after pulling her t-shirt off, baring her lovely rosé-colored nipples.

"I'll make sure to transfer your personal data off to another unit…" Leah said, smiling as she watched Apolina's fascination grow at watching Eden kiss her way down Joker's neck, chest, and abdomen.

Eden removed her gray lacy boy shorts and gave them to Joker who put them to his face and inhaled her musky feminine fragrance. Her scent shot straight to his manhood. Apolina stared as Eden pulled off his black silk pajama bottoms and boxers in one swoop. Apolina had heard many EIE dancers in the past talk about Joker Red's legendary manhood size. Her mouth watered at the sight of it. He was so hair-free down there that she just knew it got sucked on a lot because women couldn't resist a huge dick and balls with no hair around to choke them. Even the new rescue girl- Ariel- was correct in her description of it curved and looked like it was a big python wrapping itself across his waist when he laid on his back.

Apolina didn't want to leave but since she wasn't invited, she felt awkward. "I was goin' down to the beach to tan so I'll see you later about the um…phone and data."

Leah watched the hot little 5 feet 2-inch Panamanian goddess walk away as Eden sat in his lap and slowly slid her wet pussy juices all along the stalk of his immense length. After he laid back on the bed, she was on top with her bald pussy open, shiny with her morning dew, her tiny star like pink anus visible.

Leah watched Apolina's phat tattooed buttocks slowly jiggle and sway sexily as she made her way to the door. That bikini she wore was all-black but was useless when it came to covering up any of the "creamy coffee" colored 20-year-old Central American in the front; she may as well as been wearing a postage stamp and in the back, her ass crack had swallowed the rest.

"Apple," Leah stopped her. "We call it *the beast*."

"Huh?"

"Our Daddy's dick." Leah grinned. "Its name is Beast."

"It's the biggest and prettiest one I've ever seen." Apolina said as she watched Eden now slowly rubbing Joker's thick weapon all over her lovely face.

Leah stood up and walked over to Apolina saying, "You have the loveliest ass and your beauty is very exotic. Would you like to sit with me and watch?"

Apolina felt giddy as Leah led her over to one of the large sofas. Leah, who was only wearing a short red Prada teddy, sat very close to Apolina. She almost immediately started talking dirty to the sexy Panamanian. "You see how she places her face all along the underside of his meat and pushes her nose softly into his sack?"

Apolina had one foot up on the couch and the other down on the floor. "Yeah I see."

"She's smelling his scent," Leah revealed.

"Mmm." Apolina's knee started to sway left and right to help with the pulsing feeling she was feeling inside of her vagina. "How's his smell?"

"Like a hot and sexy man," Leah said as she traced the flag of Panama tattoo on Apolina's neck. "His pre-cum is like your sweetest lip gloss… or your favorite chocolate and caramel salty sweet snack. You just want more."

Eden handled his beast with both hands. One milked his large balls while the other helped her guide him in and out of her hot wet mouth.

"Your pussy's wet like crazy right now, huh?" Leah asked Apolina as Eden started easing the beast into her throat.

Apolina nodded. "A puddle. I'm so wet… You?"

"Can I help?" Leah asked her.

Apolina nodded.

Leah first stood up and undressed. Apolina's eyes seemed to devour Leah's thick body. She noticed wetness on Leah's labia and the scent of her caused Apolina to come up out of her own bikini. Leah pushed Apolina back and spread out on top of her.

"You a bad, bad bitch, Apple," Leah declared and tongue kissed the Panamanian vixen as if she was her girlfriend. "Gimme that sweet tongue, girl."

Leah suckled her neck while locking her wet pussy against her hip. Leah turned all of her attention to Apolina's lovely breasts and elongated nipples. While Leah humped her pussy on Apolina's left hip and thigh, leaving a wet trail, Apolina humped back and watched Eden who was now on all fours with her face in the mattress being slowly fucked by her husband.

Only- by this time- Valerie, Coral, Iani, Uzenna, Ashley, and Brittani were all awake and enjoying the show. Ashley grabbed the scented oil and started sensually massaging Eden. Valerie followed suit and started in on Eden's back. Iani and Uzenna used the oil on Joker and did the same for him rubbing it into his back, buttocks, and hamstring muscles. Eden pulled Coral Nee in front of her and opened up the shapely China girl's white legs. Eden moaned and sobbed from all of the pleasure she was receiving as Joker sawed his thick foot long cucumber in and out of her while Ashley was mindful enough to find her erect clitoris during her sensual and loving massage of her belly and breasts.

"I'm cummin', ohh my God… I'm cumin' all over that big juicy beast, Daddy." Eden cried out and punched a fist down on the mattress. "Mm… c'mere. White China, let me taste you baby."

What had started out as something that would probably be over quick turned into one of the most loveliest things Apolina had ever seen. Joker Red had all of these beautiful young wives around him and he made love to all of them. He did stop briefly to go pee but when he returned, he did have a glass of water in his hand, and it looked to Apolina like he'd taken something. Viagra perhaps? Whatever it was, it worked because for the next several hours, he fucked all of his wives.

"I want my whole body to smell like your cunt when we're done," Leah said as she ate Apolina's fragrant pussy.

Joker was on the bed drenched in perspiration as he savagely fucked Ashley. "Open them pretty ass legs wider, baby, and gimme that tight pussy," he whispered into the lovely brunette's ear.

"It's open, Daddy, I'm so open for you." Ashley whimpered as she whipped her pussy in maddening circles. "Oooh, shiiittt… cuummm-miiinnnn' again."

"I need to be fucked so bad," Apolina whined as she mashed her pussy all up in Leah's face.

Leah already had three fingers inside of the sweaty little vixen's pussy. "Don't move." Leah commanded her.

"You gonna share her or what Lee?" Iani asked.

"Hell yeah," Leah nodded. "Go get strapped up. We gonna give it to this bitch."

Leah grabbed some Astro Glide lube, some pillows and towels, and called Apolina to follow her into the women's shoe closet. There were two red velvet sofas inside of the enormous room. The size of the closet if compared to where Iani and Leah had originally came from was sickening to think of. The opulence of the palatial rooms was beyond belief.

Leah looked at Iani who had put on an expensive 8-inch black strap on dildo. The design was made for the woman who was wearing it to receive maximum pleasure because it had a fatter, shorter end that was inside of Iani and a clitoral tickler that would stimulate her as she fucked Apolina.

"You'll have her asshole and Imma fist-bang her pussy," Leah told Iani. "We about to blow your lights out, Apple. You ain't cum yet til' you had what we about to give you."

In the bedroom, Joker was staring at Valerie as he stroked her slippery, wet depths long. She clenched her teeth and left bite marks on his arms and scratches on his back. She couldn't help it because of how deep he went inside of her so Joker held both of her arms high above her head.

"Mm, the rape position, Daddy, ooooooooouuuuuuu, Fuck. Don't let it slip out again." Valerie yelled at him. "Hold my hands high and take my white pussy! Take it. Rape me! Daddy! Ohh, shit, go harder!"

She brought her long legs up and clasped them behind his back. Every time he went in and out of her, wet slick noises could be made. Uzenna, Ashley, Coral, Eden, and Brittani were on both sides of the copulating couple, tantalizing Joker with their wicked oily fingers, touching them shamelessly, grabbing his beast, and stroking his balls as Apolina stared.

Leah sucked her clit and fisted Apolina to the same exact tempo that Iani used to thrust the big 8-inch dildo deep inside of her. Iani started going faster and she used the dildo's remote control to turn the vibrator on. Soon, Iani began to crash into a mind-blowing orgasm.

"Hard! Fuck me hard!" Apolina screamed as the two women did exactly that. "Fist my pussy. Ohhh Fuck…it gonna…. OOOOUUUU-UUU. AAAAAIIIIIIEEEEEEE!! C-C-CUUMMIIIING."

When they were done, Apolina was breathing hard as if she had asthma or had run a marathon.

"You want some of her, Daddy?" Leah asked as she removed her hand from Apolina's still pulsating vagina. "She the hottest little fuckin' thing."

"Nah." Joker said, turning her down. "I'm cool wit the women I love and who have given me children. Y'all play wit all the babes y'all want… I ain't puttin' my meat in none of 'em no more. Who still tryna fuck?"

They all went back in the room to continue.

Iani and Leah stayed with Apolina.

CHAPTER THIRTY-ONE

Ghostman & Honey B
Ontario, CA
2:50 AM

Honey B sat up in the middle of the night cradling hers and Ghostman's new son, Petey. She couldn't sleep and obviously the baby couldn't either, so she gave him a bread stick to gnaw on while she did some thinking.

"B?" Ghostman called for her in the dark with his hand gripping the AR-15 next to his head.

"I'm up with baby," she called from the baby's nursery.

They were not in Winthrop Harbor, Illinois. They owned another even greater mansion and estate in Ontario, California. It was a modernized 60- room home filled with glazed Italian marble floors and walls and it could even be seen built into the exterior sides of the fortress. It was solar powered and filled with ceiling fans in each room to help keep it cool in the summer.

Ghostman looked at his phone and could see that it was 2:20AM. He threw on a black designer sweat suit, laced up his gray and black

201

Nike Lebron 18 Lows, and walked into the nursery with his AR-15 strapped to his back, sitting down on the sofa.

"I don't know what to do," Honey revealed in an unusually small, unauthoritative voice.

"No?" He replied. "Any other time you'd have all the answers."

She rolled her eyes at him. "Why don't you just go on back in the room and do what you been doin'… *nothing*."

"I'm bout tired of your fuckin' mouth," Ghostman cautioned her.

Caustic anger was inside both of their guts like phosphorous fire raining down from the night skies like Putin's war which they had started with Joker Red, but they needed each other. The Albanians only trusted in what they both brought to the table. Ghostman had financed the takeover plan and thus far, it was yielding "very comfortable" results.

On the other hand, Honey B's Mexican Drug Cartel connections were happy. They were, once more, moving massive amounts of Fentanyl, heroin, cocaine, and crystal methamphetamine in Chicago but not at the level they wanted to reach by now. Especially not with a trained private military company like EIE still around taking out cartel management with the green light of the federal government. It was unfathomable what the FBI was allowing to take place on American streets.

Joker Red and the EIE Army were no better than any other common criminal or gangsters in the street, yet they acted with impunity, actually killing off other criminals to push the EIE agenda ahead.

This was unprecedented. Never before had the feds turned a blind eye to such wholesale killings of people… well maybe not since the FBI used to allow racist groups like the Ku Klux Klan to get away with murdering Blacks during the Civil Rights struggle. Anyone who saw the movie *Mississippi Burning* knows about that. And niggas haven't forgotten it.

"I don't know whether to hope… or despair," she stated, sounding lost.

There was a short pause. "Better learn how to do both… fuckin' wit that nigga."

She laid their son back down since he'd nodded back off. "Meanin' what?"

"He won't kill no kid but he'd arrange it, so you thought he did," Ghost enlightened her. "He did after that fuckin' nigga Khadafi killed Joker's brother, Al. I think that's what did Khadafi in. Joker had broken him mentally."

"Why would he take my son Victor and his nanny?" She asked. "I had them hidden far away – on another continent."

Ghostman laughed. "First off, the nigga got CIA and DOD juice now. He make a phone call and get satellite images of shit Google Earth can't see. Killin' him was the only chance and now…"

Ghostman just let the thought hang.

"And now?" She repeated.

"Your nanny's dead," Ghostman told her. "No need to keep her around… I bet a dollar against a dime that ya son is on the EIE airbase. He too smart to keep Hector with him."

"I'm wondering if we can expose this secret vigilante program they got," Honey B suggested. "Take what we know to the media."

Ghostman got up and escorted her back to their own master bedroom. "Are you fuckin' nuts? You do that and then the CIA will pull a Jimmy Hoffa on you, me, your son, and anyone else we know, love, or care for."

She googled Jimmy Hoffa while sitting on the side of their bed. "*Missing Teamsters union boss feared dead,*" she muttered.

"Never found his bones," Ghostman said.

"That ain't just dead, that's Mafia Dead."

He scanned the security monitors which were mounted into the wall next to the wall-mounted 70-inch HDTV. He saw his armed guards on the outer perimeter manning their posts with machine guns at the ready.

"Could they indict us if they wanted to?"

Ghostman pondered her question as she laid down across the bed on her stomach with her head in his lap. "No. I was EIE when Red's lawyer Mecca Montecristo got it in writing that all of us were immune from being prosecuted for all known and unknown crimes."

"*Up to that date*," she pointed out. Then she seemed to speak in a lower octave. "We need a very worthy sacrifice, an extremely high-priced…"

He pushed her gently off of him. "I agree. If you call Joker now and renounce Hector as your son, he'll have no power over us."

She stared daggers at him. "Have you lost your mind?"

"You've kept that boy away from me so don't look at me as if I should love him as my son," he shot at her.

"So." She snapped, standing up. "That means you'll be more willin' to kill him? I hid him to-"

"Blackmail me, bitch." He stood up and faced her. "You've held those tapes on me of Esmeralda Cartegena and Daphne Jessoms to force me into doing your bidding. Theses mad plans of yours and you hid your son to keep me from reversing those plans by kidnapping him or killin' him myself."

"The tapes have been erased you asshole!" She screamed at him. "At first, they weren't, I admit that… I used them as leverage to get what I want."

"Leverage, blackmail are the same cloth," he stated as he opened up the balcony doors. "I wouldn't have spent five million dollars on your Albanian plans if -"

"Exactly," she said. "Now we have ten million back and another thirty-five million in product. We'd have probably more in cash if you bought less cars."

He blew her off with a smirk on his face. "These properties you selected cost just as much as my cars."

"Doesn't matter. We don't make money to look at it," she said. "But if I didn't do what I did, you'd still be eating the crumbs Joker left behind for you. As for Hector… he was hidden more out of fear of El Verdugo's enemies coming back for revenge."

"So why didn't you hide with him?"

She shook her head. "A mother lioness or fox always leads danger away from her cubs."

He went out onto the balcony which gave them a steep view overlooking the ritzy city they now lived, to the right and to the left he could see upwards at the San Bernadino Mountains. He rolled up a blunt of Kush and lit it up.

"Ay," he called back to her.

She walked out in the warm night air.

"I ain't want you to throw ya son under the axe," he said.

"I know."

"*Kits.*"

She looked puzzled. "Huh?"

"Foxes," he stated. "They don't have cubs. They have kits. A mother fox is called a —"

"Vixen," she finished for him.

He toked from the blunt and gave it to her. While she smoked from it he bent down and reached underneath her Chanel gown. She thought he was just going for a feel of her luscious ass cheeks, but he grabbed her panties and pulled them down.

"Um mm," she murmured around the blunt between her lips. "Don't... I'm bleeding, Papi."

He pulled them off anyway. "So?" He held the black silk thong panties up to his nose and inhaled her aromatic feminine scent.

"You are so dirty..." She whispered. "There's a blood scent there?"

She touched him and felt how hard he'd become.

"Speaking of blood..." he trailed off, pulling her along with him. "I was thinkin' we need a significant sacrifice too."

"Two chickens?" She asked.

He shook his head. "Get dressed."

She changed into jeans, a t-shirt, and sneakers. She told the nanny she was leaving and followed her husband out into the large aluminum custom-built work shed. He turned on the light, closed the door behind them, and made sure that it was locked.

An enormous green Tupperware trunk sat inside of the shed. The top had holes drilled into it and it was sealed with duct tape. Honey B turned down the radio that was sitting on top of the wooden work table.

Ghostman gave his wife an orange box cutter and pointed at the trunk. "Cut around the tape. Open it."

Honey B hesitated. "It has breathing holes in it, Papi. Is this the chickens?"

"Chickens ain't enough," Ghostman said. "Bigger."

"A goat?"

"Just open it, scared ass bitch."

"You a scared ass bitch," she countered. "Does it have teeth? Just tell me that. Fang teeth."

"Teeth, yeah. Fangs, no."

"Okay." She began cutting the tape. "No fangs so no venom."

She cut the tape and then removed the lid. What she saw shocked her. She stood back and stared.

"It's a *girl*!" She said with her mouth open.

"Behold, our sacrifice. A *virgin* sacrifice."

They slit the girl's throat while reading verses from the Satanic Bible.

CHAPTER THIRTY-TWO

Meth Man Ace
The Jasper Plantation
Jasper, Florida

Meth Man Ace and his wives abandoned their plans to drop anchor in Kissimmee, Florida because there was entirely too much activity going on. Orlando, a tourist attraction for example, was barely a stone's throw away. So, they located a massive plantation in northern Florida just south of the border in Jasper. The land they now owned was purported to once be a thriving slave plantation.

The 25-room colonial- style house that came with the property had only been built twenty years prior. The previous owners had farmed oranges and other produce from the land but once they died, their children had chosen to sell their inheritance off. Meth Man had Mecca Montecristo help close the deal and Jasper was where he now set up shop.

The house was outstanding. It was a gold stucco with white beams. The main driveway was done with all gold bricks. The renovators had very little to do since the sellers had already thought much of what needed fixed over very thoroughly.

Surrounded by creeks such as the Alapaha and the Okefenokee Swamp, irrigation would not be the problem. In fact, Meth Man preferred the cover of big cypress trees, snakes, and alligators. Outsiders would think twice about sneaking in. In other words, there was a dark side to the land where many of its acres would be used to create crystal methamphetamines and also Fentanyl.

Each meth lab and Fentanyl lab were set up inside of the swamp on house boats.

"The beauty of these…" Meth had told his wives, "… is that each are rigged to be remote detonated any time we need 'em to be."

"I just don't like them loud ass air boats," Natalya told him when he showed them.

"How else we gon' get to 'em?" Meth Man had reasoned. "Swim?"

"I see the strategy," Blanca told him. "But I don't like the air boats either. They're so loud."

"So, hey…" he spoke to his wives once they were officially moved into the Jasper Plantation. "Y'all like Yajaira's brother?"

"Why you bring him up?" Bambina wanted to know.

"Cuz y'all didn't," he accused them.

"He was fun," Natalya said. "Period."

"Why you thinkin' about Yajaira?" Bambina queried.

He nodded. "She stood out."

All four of his wives scoffed.

"She's an *exotic Brazilian*," Natalya pointed out. "Papi, she coulda been Venezuelan, Norwegian – or Dominican like us. She has new body, new vagina, everything. You want her again yes?"

He nodded.

Bambina slapped her hand on the dining room table where they all had been sitting for breakfast. "That's exactly why we say *one-time rule*. So, no one gets feelings."

He scratched his face. "Y'all right. I'm blockin' her number."

〜

The CIN Offices
West Palm Beach, FL

JOKER RED HAD EVERYONE ON HIS CHECKLIST TRANSPORTED TO THE Central Intelligence Network at 10:00 AM. It was time to get down to business. The entire basement floor had been built for "War Room" and conference activity, so it easily held everyone.

"I need to talk to you." Nina whispered to Joker just prior to the start of the epic meeting.

Joker was standing by the coffee table stirring up a large cup of black Bustelo Coffee. "Spit it Nee, we gotta make it pop."

"Outside," she told him.

They stepped out into the hallway and was joined by Maxine Crawford from the Department of Defense and Nyomi Malek of the FBI.

"We brought our own people on for support," Nina revealed. "They're upstairs now but their identities must be kept secret so-"

"You mean they're wearing face masks," Joker said it plainly. "Why? We got it under control."

"Nobody said you didn't," Maxine cut in.

"We're not just going out to California and Chicago to help you 'neutralize' everybody," Nyomi added. "We need to make a big statement."

"You mean the FBI," Joker said.

"The fuckin' federal government," Maxine stated emphatically.

Joker stared the older white woman in her deathly gray eyes. "You turn me loose one minute the next you bring in- what – babysitters, Now…faceless *Sicarios*?"

Nyomi explained the FBI plan better. "We're shutting down the Albanians in a nationwide raid and turning them over to ICE. We know that you have your eyes on Ghostman Stevens, his wife, and probably some others. We can't risk him making it into a courtroom, so you'll have them. The faceless *Sicarios* that are coming in are not hitmen, Joker Red. They're the best field commanders in the agency, S.W.A.T. personnel, ready to order other ground troops to synchronize their watches and hit these fuckers hard."

Joker nodded. "Aight, let 'em in."

CHAPTER THIRTY-THREE

The CIN Meeting
West Palm Beach, FL

The FBI S.W.A.T. personnel came into the CIN dressed down in various civilian wear. They did have sidearms and badges to identify themselves as agents but none of their names were visible. They didn't talk, nor did they even wish to be spoken to. They all stood around the conference tables and chairs that were set up.

Nyomi dug right on into the meeting. "We're goin' to listen to a recording first of an exchange between Ghostman Steven Adams, Senior and his …wife?"

Nina, who was sitting down at one of the tables, replied, "Yes. Beatrice Lourdes Mendes-Diaz aka Honey B."

Nyomi nodded and played the recording over the HDTV's speakers.

Honey B: *"What happened?"*

Ghostman: *"Boom."*

Honey B: *"Did we get the main one?"*

Ghostman: *"Fucker wasn't even there. Whole shit got me fuckin' pissed off cuz those was my war comrades."*

Honey B: *"No more talkin' just get home. We'll regroup."*

Joker looked puzzled as did Uzenna, Bible, and other EIE members who were aware of the car bombings early last year at the Hummer dealership. Killed were Joker's wives: Louise, Melodie, Diane, Julia, and children: Stephanie, Justin, Francesa, Afton, and EIE warriors: Monk, Black N9NE, Big Chief, Fast Eddie, Mustafa, and Ground War.

"What's the date on that recording?" Joker cut in. "Cuz I never heard it."

"We demanded the same thing when we heard it," Nyomi explained. "It was actually captured by one of those NSA sweeps the same day of the event."

"No one heard it til' recently?" Joker queried.

Nyomi nodded. "NSA does millions of these illegal sweeps every day and no one put two and two together until one of their young data analysts came across it because of the word *'boom'*."

Leah, sitting behind him, put a calming hand on his shoulder.

Nyomi used a handheld device to publish digital photos on the wall-to-ceiling large screen. "The recording goes on very shortly thereafter where Adams and Mendes-Diaz implicate a co-conspirator named only 'Vee' Most everyone here knows that we have procured one hundred and fifteen warrants to arrest, search and seize, nationwide. Steven Ghostman Adams, his wife Mendes- Diaz, Victoria Linze- better known as Valoria Linze – will be transported by EIE, Inc. Personnel to their airbase, questioned and … moving on."

Nyomi published the photos of Ghostman, Honey B, and Valoria/Victoria Linze.

"As we know, since we've been bugging them for some time now, Valoria has a wide web of associates on our radar," Nyomi stated and published one photo after the other. Each time she did so, a paper copy was generated with related warrant information on each individual. "Namely an Albanian counterfeit documents expert Lazar Maras and Kolya Moroz. They're a very dangerous pair who own a dry cleaner on Central Boulevard, Los Angeles. They have been supplying Valoria and an Albanian Mafia organization named The One or NJË in their own language and the docs are so well done, it strikes fear into the hearts of CBP and HSA agents on the watch for suspected terrorists who could try to enter the U.S. on an airplane. We will arrest, prosecute, and dismantle their network. It is because of them that we have been able to identify all of those The One members who are here illegally."

She paused to publish dozens of individual Albanian mobsters in Valoria's organization.

"They're awfully smart," Nyomi said. "For every strip club EIE opened to create revenue for PMC missions, the Albanians opened a tattoo shop nearby. Sometimes directly across the street. While doing so they have been using sex slaves to promote Mexican Drug Cartel - bought crystal methamphetamines, fentanyl-laced heroin, and cocaine from Los Angeles, all throughout the Mid-West and up and down the East Coast. In fact, Sergeant David Hodges, a former Army Ranger… can you please stand up?"

Joker stood up and looked at the twenty plus faceless FBI personnel standing along the room's walls. The he retook his seat.

"Sergeant David Hodges likes it better if we call him Joker Red," Nyomi introduced him. "He's CEO and Commanding Officer of EIE, Inc. Anyway, his wife Leah Hodges (Leah stands, then sits.) is the tech nerd of the EIE family. She sleuths around and locates what the FBI could not."

The face of Rose Rice Donohue popped up on the screen followed by two others.

"Rose Rice Donohue," Nyomi said. "Joker Red, Big Eustace 'Bible' Reed (Bible stands, then sits), and Agent Overstreet of the CIA bursts into a Las Vegas hotel room and locates Rose Rice Donohue, Kalani Muhammad, and Ariel Montoya who were being sex trafficked by Albanians. The power structure starts in New York under a man named Alexei Biederman aka 'Mad Wolf' who control sex trafficking and narcotics in the East and he has a man on the West Coast named Georg Knoerkl aka Nuri according to the rescued girl Montoya."

During a break, Joker was joined by Don Braga, Vinnie, and several others in his fourth-floor office.

"I feel outta place here," Vinnie spoke with a shrug.

"The faceless guys standin' around are makin' me uncomfortable," Don Braga added. "Kinda reminds me of me except I'd have the mask and we'd be throwin' the black hood over somebody's head!"

The two brothers laughed.

"This is political theatre," Joker told them. "Since EIE, Inc. is now a PMC this is what I have to get used to listening to. We have a mercenary army of five maybe six hundred tops. With the right training facility and equipment, we can overthrow small governments. But we aren't at that level."

Joker sat down behind the desk.

"I was directed to invite all of my allies here," Joker admitted.

"By who?" Don Braga asked him.

"CIA, DOD," Joker answered.

"But why?" Vinnie wanted to understand.

"You sit atop a billion-dollar organization," Joker told them. "Cocaine, heroin, fentanyl, crystal methamphetamine business in Chicago- America's heartbeat. They know us... They're tired of the chaos the Mexican Drug Cartels bring."

Nina entered the room. "Don Frank, Don Vincent," she nodded their way.

They acknowledged her.

"Everybody out except the Bragas," Joker said.

The office cleared.

"Next time y'all want the Bragas to get a message, don't use me to do it," Joker stated vehemently.

Nina sighed and flopped down on the sofa. "It made perfect sense, Red. But we weren't the ones who let them in on our deal. *You* were and *you* were heard on a wiretap discussing it."

Joker's eyes narrowed.

Nina crossed her legs. "Don Frank... Do we have to spell it all out for you? There's a special prosecutor in Chicago this instant whose been investigating Mafia activities and can stick you and your brother with RICO charges."

Don Frank laughed and lit a cigar. "Whattaya want from me? To join your Assassination Program?"

"Give it whatever name you want," Nina told him. "We just believe in using fire to put out fire because water doesn't always work. Why not use the biggest and baddest to stomp out others who're big and bad? I'll tell you what, how about you set up one of the biggest gun buyback programs your city has ever seen and guarantee two hundred dollars for every workable firearm? Other than that, when this PMC needs it, you loan soldiers. You do that and that special prosecutor will return to D.C."

"I'm a businessman," Don Braga told Nina. "Deal."

"We're about to move out with Alpha Team, Joker," Nina informed him, standing up and making her way over to the bar Leah had so craftily set up in the office. She poured herself a shot of tequila. "Mind if I take the bottle?"

"Help yourself," Joker told her.

"In that case," she remarked. "I'll take two."

She walked out after that.

Joker looked at Frank Braga. "You gave in kinda easy there."

Frank sighed and clasped his big fingers as he sat down on the expensive office sofa. "Runnin' a national criminal empire is hard enough without these bastards breathing down our necks. That's why I've distanced us from so many criminal rackets. But I've sat – we've sat (indicating Vinnie) – on the sideline watching you and your people not be touched with one indictment for all this time."

"I told Frank it'd never work," Vinnie admitted. "I wondered if they'd make youse into rats, testifying for them, but... I just didn't get it."

"*What?*" Joker's face turned ugly.

"Calm down, they're the government – feds." Frank held up a hand. "But we didn't see no hammer come down for the Chicago 80 Hit List. Them fuckers knew youse were ex-military and decided, '*hey we can use their combined military mastery with criminal mastery, but we need to benefit.*' So, the very second they said they'd call their dog off- the special prosecutor – I knew I'd be okay. See that tells me that our organization is no longer national but international."

"The Feds run the borders," Vinnie stated. "That means the shipping ports from Miami to Boston Harbor are ours. Vancouver to Los Angeles. We can buy a hundred million dollars in low-priced pharmaceutical opiate medicine. Pills from the Swiss and make eight hundred million on the street. We give them a hundred million … and kill terrorists, spies, pedophiles, sex traffickers, and serial killers?"

Don Frank inhaled and exhaled. "We're their executioners, Joker. They own us now. Are you okay with that?"

Joker Red opened up a box of Havana cigars. "Drug dealing, medicine, smuggling, law enforcement, lawyering, killing, or oil. They're all dirty businesses. Plus, I've made it clear to these fuckers if you call us, we ain't into lining mufuckaz up for prosecution. We come to help the weak and kill everyone else involved. You gotta find a way to atone for all the blood, Don Frank. That's how I sleep at night."

They went back down to the meeting.

CHAPTER THIRTY-FOUR

The CIN Meeting

Once the meeting adjourned and all of the raid plans were in place, Joker stayed seated in the room with only his wives, Bible, Nina, and Nyomi.

"I don't like it," Joker protested.

Leah pushed a large suitcase across the table to Nina which she immediately opened, examined the contents, and closed it. The suitcase was just another under-the-table payment to the CIA.

"The money pay off?" Nyomi inquired.

"Fuck money, I ain't talkin' about that," he said. "Louise, Melodie, Diane, Julia, our three daughters Stephanie, Frannie, and Afton. My son Justin. My fuckin' comrades Monk, N9NE, Chief, Eddie, Staf, and Ground War. All I can think of is seeing their bodies. Ghostman, Honey B, and Valoria conspired with others to plant those bombs. They had mercury triggers and parts in 'em only them Albanians use."

Nina glanced at Nyomi and Nyomi admitted, "We sent him the results from the FBI lab in D.C. He's right. The wire circuitry, high tech bomb components, the primers, and a smokeless gunpowder… all foreign materials. What don't you like?"

"Delivering Ghostman, Honey B, and Valoria ain't enough," he said.

"What do you want?" She asked.

"I want everyone involved in those fuckin' bombings," he demanded. "Y'all talkin' 'bout indictments. I ain't wit none of that shit. How y'all even got evidence for those murders in the first place? That one recording? How's that implicate a dozen other Albanians who conspire to pull off something like that?"

Nyomi shook her head. "No… no… no… no… no. We don't have the evidence for the bombings, but we do have enough for a CCE and RICO prosecution. There'll be no bond. If you want revenge in any other way…well, their new address won't be private. You know what you'll have to do."

"So, I'll know where they'll be held?" Joker asked. "You sure?"

"My word is on it." Nyomi shook Joker's hand. "We all have planes to catch."

"C'mon, Bible, we rollin'," Joker said as they all exited. He hugged and kissed his wives. "Don't worry. It ain't even our show. They got the bigger army this time."

"At least you'll get to – we'll get to avenge their deaths," Uzenna said, holding onto the lapels of his tac jacket. "I'm proud of you, Daddy."

"All of us are," Leah repeated the same.

On the way to the airport there was a small change in plans, and it was decided that Ariel Montoya should travel with Team Bravo: Nina would be on that team which, thus far, consisted of Joker Red, Bible, one of the "faceless" FBI SWAT commanders, and herself.

"She'll know the Las Vegas strip better than we do in case Nuri goes mobile or even disappears," Nina reasoned as their black GMC passenger van motored in the direction of the estate.

"I thought your guys were sittin' on him." Joker looked back at the faceless agent.

"We are," was all he said and offered no more.

Picking up Ariel set them back an extra hour because she had to pack. Then, on the flight out to Vegas – on a C- 130 of all things – Joker had to calm her fears of actually having to face the sex traffickers. She felt like she was betraying them when it was they who were *the real* evil.

CHAPTER THIRTY-FIVE

Team Bravo
Sunrise Manor, Nevada

There were three primary teams: Team Alpha, Team Bravo, and Team Charlie. All three had clear objectives.

Team Alpha: Apprehend Ghostman and Honey B at their new mansion on Euclid Avenue in Ontario, California and then travel to Los Angeles to apprehend Valoria. The three were to be transported to the EIE, Inc. airbase in Custer, South Dakota, where Joker Red would have them on a silver platter. The type that was served cold.

Team Bravo: Was in Las Vegas to free as many sex slaves as possible out of the 200 that Ariel Montoya had reported knowing about and seeing during her own enslavement. Also, the FBI wanted to apprehend Nuri and dismantle the entire Albanian criminal network that was operating in Sin City's child sex/sex trade.

Team Charlie: Would be apprehending Nuri's boss in New York, Mad Wolf, and dismantling his sex trafficking network.

All of the EIE, Inc. personnel were assigned to two dozen other teams throughout the country to assist the "faceless" SWAT Commanders in taking out the Mexican Drug Cartels who have been … identified in supporting Honey B and Valoria's NJË organization. For example, Bushwacker and Boo were sent to Arizona to assist in hunting down Tijuana Drug Cartel members:

Helena Jaramillo

Laila Jaramillo

Nobi Jaramillo

Another team in Dallas- Fort Worth was there to hunt down Nico Gonzalez, Aurelio Reyes, Juan Baez, and Julio "Kiko" Romero-Villegas of the Gulf Drug Cartel. According to intelligence gathered by the DEA both the Tijuana and Gulf Drug Cartels had been bank-rolling the Albanians and also assisting them in smuggling into the U.S. some of the most dangerous Albanian criminals. Some of which were connected to known smugglers of "radioactive" materials used to make dirty bombs. Breach and Goliath were assigned to this particular hunt.

All the other teams were scattered all throughout the infamous Meth Alley State to hit all of the Albanian tattoo shops which had been erected nearby all of EIE, Inc's strip clubs. The NJË's grand conspiracy had been to set up tattoo shops next to each club and siphon off money by using Mexican Drug Cartel- bought methamphetamines, heroin, cocaine, and fentanyl. There was no doubt their plan had been working. The EIE set up was easily bringing in about $20 million per month from all of the combined "Meth Alley" States: Nebraska, Kansas, Iowa, Illinois, Missouri, Indiana, Kentucky, and Tennessee.

Ghostman and Honey B were cutting into the EIE bottom line by nearly $5 million per month according to Leah and Uzenna's numbers. That meant less "suitcases full of cash" to the CIA and that simply would not be tolerated. Joker knew that the loss of the money could certainly be the catalyst behind the decision for this massive "nation-wide sweep" underway.

They landed at Nellia Air Force Base which was located North of Las Vegas. From there they were transported by Apache helicopter to a large ranch outside of Sunrise Manor. It was a fifteen-acre property procured by Uzenna via Air BNB.

"They're here already," the faceless FBI SWAT Commander pointed at the 16-man squad that's awaited them when they disembarked from the Apache.

Joker, Bible, Nina, and Ariel were all introduced to the elite team of FBI SWAT Unit. They wore masks to conceal their faces. Over the next 90 minutes the entire group met inside of the barn where their command post was set up and they went over plans.

"We have approximately thirty-two hours until strike time," the Commander said. "Report back in twenty-four hours. Dismissed."

The "faceless" agents left the ranch including the Commander. Nina, Bible, Joker, and Ariel had fast food delivered with a large Instacart order. They ate, showered in their own bathrooms, and prepared for bed.

Nina knocked on Joker's door. She had on a white jogging suit that said Fendi on the hoody. "Can I come in, Red?"

"Come on," he told her.

"What you doing? She asked him.

"Havin' a by myself meetin'," he replied.

"About what?"

"This mistake y'all makin'," he mentioned.

"How's it a mistake? We're rounding these bastards up and -"

"Half of 'em will beat the charges," Joker cut her short. "Now I'm not even with puttin' niggas in cuffs no matter who it is. You know what I do already. I'm sayin' it's a mistake because these fuckers is gonna eventually make a way back and then I got another mufucka out there wit a rifle aimed at me or my loved ones."

"So, execute them all?" Nina questioned. "You know we can't do that."

Joker, who was laying on the bed, shirtless, sat up. His skin gleamed from the shower water and scented baby oil he used, and it sent a pulse down to her clit. She sat next to him.

"Y'all had told me to stall after the mufucka tried to have me poisoned and that *Fast and Furious* shit on the fuckin' highway," he said angrily. "But even before that... the bombings. Y'all said play the long game. Wait. My wives. My babies. My comrades…blown to death. Y'all got me in fuckin' Nevada supportin' this shit?"

Nina had no words to sooth his pain. She never truly considered how wounded he still was over those terrible losses.

"Listen to me, Red," she said, moving closer, holding his hand, and touching his face. "I've grown very close to you. But you know that, right?"

He nodded. "I know. Me, too."

"Then trust me. Not Nina the CIA but Nina. Me. You have been given a magnificent opportunity and power very few are given." She paused. "You have a PMC because you are remarkable. You put together a hand of loyal brother and sister soldiers who'd once served in the U.S. military. Many of you are exceptional at what you do and know. In the same way that we hire computer hackers who steal sensitive secrets or millions of dollars from banks… you have been selected to lead your PMC soldiers into the Big Picture. It's never gonna make sense. At the end of the day, hate it or love it, the U.S. is the most powerful country on earth. You'll have your revenge on those who bombed your family and soldier comrades. Just remember you are the CEO of a new PMC and as Commander, you are going to have to make Big Picture choices. *National Security* choices."

He laid back down and she snuggled in next to him. He held her all night as they slept. When she went the bathroom, she returned naked. Joker immediately pulled her sweet-scented dark chocolate colored body to him and held her tightly. He rubbed all over her breasts, nipples standing hard at attention, he squeezed her ass…kissed her neck. He even had her laid out on her stomach and went down to kiss her all inside of her ass crack, smelling all in the interiors of her most precious parts, but he moaned and stopped.

"What, baby?" She whispered, reaching out to feel his beast. He was harder than a battering ram.

He just enveloped her in his muscled arms and spooned her. "Let's just sleep, Nina."

"You hard as hell, how we gonna sleep?" She inquired.

"I just wanna sleep with my wives," he told her. "You know I'm tempted cuz you feel it. You see it. But after Tithi, I'm good."

Nina fell asleep in his arms and though they wanted each other, they didn't make love. In Nina's mind, his desire to be faithful to his harem of beautiful wives back home only made her want him more.

CHAPTER THIRTY-SIX

The Raids Begin
Spring Valley, Nevada
5:49 AM

Nuri and six of his henchmen were arrested at the break of dawn as planned on Wednesday. The elite FBI SWAT Unit used high-powered percussion grenades and rushed up inside of three houses in a suburb of Las Vegas called Spring Valley.

"Where's the girls, asshole?" One of the faceless SWAT agents demanded from Nuri.

"Can I question him?" Joker asked as two of the agents stood next to the open door of the black cargo van the Albanian Mafioso was thrown into.

Nina was standing there, too, her AR-15 hanging downward. "Let him at the suspect."

The FBI Commander shrugged. "Hell, go ahead. The bastard's not talking."

Joker hopped into the van after handing Bible his M-5 sub-machine gun. "Georg Knoerkl also known as Nuri, right?" Joker asked the big balding Albanian brute.

"Yeah," he answered as he sat in handcuffs.

Joker's nod said it all.

The Commander nodded back, and they cleared all of the other examination rooms offices and no one else was there. Then they went out to the dog kennels and Joker walked zombie-like by each cage.

He started to cry as he observed the deplorable conditions that all of these women were in. He just couldn't help it. His heart exploded. He looked into the eyes of one of the young white girls.

"How old are you?" He asked her.

"Fourteen," she answered in an eastern European accent. "You're the police?"

He shook his head. "I'm a soldier."

White, Black, Latina, several teenage boys who were being rented out as girls. They still had on make-up and tight jeans with cut-off tank tops to show off their slim mid-sections.

Bible found the keys on one of the dead guardsmen. Joker was overwhelmed by the stench of human waste. These cages that were made for dogs to stay in temporarily were holding between 5 and 10 humans and they had to use a bucket to urinate and defecate in. There were twenty kennels.

"I'm counting about a hundred and seventy people," Joker said to Nina and the Commander. "Ariel said there was about two hundred. Let me have Nuri and we'll find the others. In fact, let me take all of the suspects to the ranch and I'll get every slave they have out there on the street."

Nina looked at the Commander and shrugged.

"What about the warrants?" The Commander was concerned. He knew that Nuri and his six goons would be executed.

"What about them *girls and women*?" Joker frowned. "And the boys they turned into Twinkies? You gon' really let them have three hots and a cot, medical care, and all that other comfort a jail cell got? Like hot runnin' water and a toilet?"

"Sgt. Hodges," the Commander started. "I respect your courage and tenacity. But what if some or even all of them victims want the chance to face their captors in court? Do you know how empowering that makes a victim feel?"

Joke had no more to say.

He gritted his teeth.

"We get them back," the Commander said as Joker walked off with Bible.

"Y'all found 'em?" Ariel asked when Joker returned later to the ranch.

He hugged the pretty teen. "Yeah. Hundred seventy-three of them were living in a dog kennel. The FBI's interrogating and finding the others now."

"You're a hero!" Ariel said, bursting into tears. "You and fuckin' Bibleman, man."

She wrapped her arms around Bible's neck and kissed his face all over. Bible smiled at her joy.

Joker sat down on the porch for a while gazing out over the fields deep in thought…

CHAPTER THIRTY-SEVEN

The EIE Airbase
Custer, South Dakota
12:45 PM

All of the other raids were a success except for six lower-level Albanian hitters still being sought in New York. Ghostman, Honey B, and the so-called Valoria were being held at the EIE airbase in South Dakota.

Over the next several days, all of the tattoo shops, stores, and homes of the Albanians that had been seized and sealed by the Feds were "mysteriously" burned to the ground.

Joker arrived at the airbase with all of his wives and more than 60 of EIE's core members. Ghostman was being held inside of a concrete, 5-foot 7 cell in the basement of the indoor firing range. Joker had Bible and Bushwacker order the Brig soldiers to escort all three prisoners out into the demolition field at high noon.

"Why dontcha fight me to the death like a real man, Red?" Ghostman shouted over his shoulder. "What a fuckin' coward! Havin' the feds raid me? With warrants and indictments and shit? You a fuckin' rat now, nigga?"

Bible slammed his fist into the back of Ghostman's head, nearly knocking him unconscious. "On your feet and quiet." Bible commanded him.

"All y'all are whores for the fuckin' CIA now!" Ghostman hollered as he was pushed into a white police cruiser and seat belted into the back seat by Bible and Bushwacker.

Valoria was placed into the rear seat, strapped in, and the door shut behind her in a separate police car. Last, Honey B was secured in a third police cruiser.

"In case anybody wondering…" Joker said loudly to everyone watching. "This is judgment day for the murderers of our EIE family members, comrades, my wives, your sisters, and our babies. Louise, Melodie, Diane, Julia, Stephanie, Justin, Francesca, Afton, Monk, Black N9NE, Big Chief, Fast Eddie, Mustafa, Ground War… and we can't forget Esmeralda Cartegena, Daphne, Jessika, and Cheekie who were all raped and murdered by Ghostman and Honey B knew about these crimes and said nothing…"

Joker looked into the car Ghostman sat in and said to him, "You are a rabid dog, and this is your day of reckoning. Each of these cars are rigged with ten pounds of C-4… right underneath your seat. Ain't that what you used to kill them with?"

"Fuck you, nigga!" Ghostman yelled at him through the window. "You'll get yours."

Joker just walked away and the digital timers in each vehicle seemed to come alive on their own accord, visible to Valoria, Honey B, and Ghostman because they were right on the dashboards of the cars they were a prisoner in.

"Joker, Joker! Please listen!" Honey B cried.

Joker bent down and looked at her.

"My children. What'll happen to?!" she started to ask.

"Fuck your children, you treacherous bitch," Joker said coldly as he walked off. Then he turned back. "You tell me where all the money is y'all stole from us and I'll take care of your kids."

She tried to beg for her life, but it was no use. So, she told Joker about the trunks of cash buried beneath the new house in Ontario. "Ghostman…he never trusted banks. We started buying gold."

"Your kids will live good lives," Joker promised her. "But yours is over in a few minutes."

He stopped briefly at Valoria's car. "All of your men involved in the bombings will die. EIE has set free nearly all those you sex trafficked. Everyone caught in the FBI net will be kicked out of the country. I have the green light to execute every fuckin' one of you Albanian Mafioso whose involved with human trafficking. No cops, no judges, *just us*."

Joker cleared all of his army back until they were at least 1000 yards away from the blast radius. Uzenna tightly gripped one of his hands and Leah his other. Even though they all stood outside of the blast radius didn't mean that they were completely immune from the devastating sounds of the three massive explosions when they final went off.

K-K-AAABOOOOOOMMMMM!!!

K-K-AAABOOOOOOMMMMM!!!

K-K-AAABOOOOOOMMMMM!!!

The fire and smoke clouds that went up were incredible. All sixty plus EIE members cheered the deaths of Ghostman, Honey B, and Valoria.

"I told y'all we'd get revenge for our people's deaths." Joker yelled. "May God bless their souls."

"God don't want shit to do wit that Satan worshippin' bastard," Uzenna said. "Leah told me the feds found evidence of human sacrifice at their house, Daddy."

Joker looked out at the blast sites.

"Yeah," he agreed. "God don't want nothin' to do with that. Y'all girls come on… lets fly on up out of here.

"What, *now*?" Bible asked as they boarded the plane.

Joker sat next to him as his sixty plus people continued to board the big C-40 Clipper.

"Bible need to talk," he said to Joker.

Joker looked at him. "What's good?"

"Bible commit murder," he confessed, a contrite look on his face.

"What, at the shelter?" Joker inquired. "That ain't shit. You did good, son. We save people's lives."

"No. Not that," Bible stated, shaking his head. "Don't be mad at me, boss. But it was Yolie. I killed Yolie."

Joker stared at Bible with a stunned look on his face. "Whattt?!" Joker whispered.

"She said the baby wasn't mine, and …"

Joker cut him off. "Don't talk no more, Bible. Just shut up about it."

"We gotta go get the body," Bible added.

Joker glared at Bible. "You left her where she can start stinkin'?"

Bible got quiet. He knew that Joker was very angry with him. Bible wondered what Joker Red was going to do next. Would he kill Bible?

Bible wondered if he should worry.

To be continued …

Hittaz 6
Coming Soon!

REVIEW

Did you enjoy the read?
Let us know how much by leaving us a review on Amazon and
Goodreads

OTHER BOOKS BY

<u>URBAN AINT DEAD</u>

Tales 4rm Da Dale

The Hottest Summer Ever

Hittin' Licks For The Holidays: Atlanta

Wet Dreams On Lockdown: The Nurse

How To Publish A Book From Prison

By **Elijah R. Freeman**

Despite The Odds

By **Juhnell Morgan**

Good Girls Gone Rogue

Good Girls Gone Rouge 2

By **Manny Black**

Hittaz

Hittaz 2

Hittaz 3

Hittaz 4

Coldhearted

Coldhearted 2

By **Lou Garden Price, Sr.**

Charge It To The Game

Charge It To The Game 2

A Summer To Remember With My Hitta

Snatched Up By A Hitta

Santa Sent Me A Real One For Christmas

Wet Dreams on Lockdown: The Unit Manager

Thug Me The Right Way 2

Thug Me The Right Way 3

Seizing A Gangsta's Heart For The Summer

Yours For The Taking

By **Nai**

A Setup For Revenge

A Setup For Revenge 2

Wet Dreams On Lockdown: The Librarian

By **Ashley Williams**

Ridin' For You

Ridin' For You, Too

Trickin' on a Heaux for Christmas: A BBW Love Story

Homie Hoppin' For The Holidays

Wet Dreams on Lockdown: The Female C.O

Letters Of His Love

By **Telia Teanna**

The State's Witness

The State's Witness 2

The State's Witness 3

This Time Won't You Save Me

This Time Won't You Save Me 2

His Summer Side Piece

By **Kyiris Ashley**

Stuck In The Trenches

Stuck In The Trenches 2

By **Huff Tha Great**

The Swipe

The Swipe 2

By **Toōla**

Melted the Heart of a Menace

Wet Dreams On Lockdown: Lieutenant Grace

By P. Wise

Merry Trapmas: Ice & Frost

By **Mia Sky**

Thug Me The Right Way

By **DiamondATL & Nai**

Atlantastan

Atlantastan 2

By **Chris Green**

IN The Streetz

IN The Streetz 2

By **Tron Hill**

Wet Dreams on Lockdown: The Male C.O

By **Tamyra Griffin**

Wet Dreams On Lockdown: The Counselor

By **Paris Iman**

Wet Dreams On Lockdown: The Warden

By **Shawnice**

Wet Dreams On Lockdown: The Captain

By **TN Jones**

Coming Soon From
<u>URBAN AINT DEAD</u>

The Hottest Summer Ever 2
THE G-CODE
Tales 4rm Da Dale 2
How To Invest In The Stock Market From Prison
By **Elijah R. Freeman**

Hittaz 6
Coldhearted 3
By **Lou Garden Price, Sr.**

The Swipe 3
By **Toola**

Good Girls Gone Rogue 3
By **Manny Black**

Despite The Odds 2
Hittin' Licks For The Holidays: Chicago
By **Juhnell Morgan**

Charge It To The Game 3
By **Nai**

Ridin' Foreva
By **Telia Teanna**

This Time Won't You Save Me 3
Healing The Heart Of A Detroit Gangsta
By **Kyiris Ashley**

BOOKS BY

URBAN AINT DEAD's C.E.O
<u>Elijah R. Freeman</u>

Triggadale

Triggadale 2

Triggadale 3

Tales 4rm Da Dale

The Hottest Summer Ever

Murda Was The Case

Murda Was The Case 2

Murda Was The Case 3

Hittin' Licks For The Holidays: Atlanta

Wet Dreams On Lockdown: The Nurse

How To Publish A Book From Prison

STAY CONNECTED

Follow
Elijah R. Freeman
On Social Media
FB: Elijah R. Freeman
IG: @the_future_of_urban_fiction